BEASTMODE 2
BLOOD IN

WITHDRAWN

JOE AWSUM

G

STREET CHRONICLES

Published by:
G Street Chronicles
P.O. Box 1822
Jonesboro, GA 30237-1822

www.gstreetchronicles.com
fans@gstreetchronicles.com

Cover Design: Hot Book Covers
                  www.hotbookcovers.com

ISBN: 978-1-9384420-9-4
LCCN: 2012942900

Join us on our social networks
Facebook
G Street Chronicles Fan Page
G Street Chronicles CEO Exclusive Readers Group
Follow us on Twitter
@GStreetChronicl

Acknowledgements

First, I'd like to thank God for making this all possible. Second, I want to give special thanks to my entire family for never giving up on me through all my trial and tribulations: Roshell Hasty, Shareana Terry, Kaimari Jones, Marcus Hasty Jr., Harmony "Moo-Moo" Hasty, Heaven "Suga Bear" Hasty, Gregory Hasty, Karla Hasty, Big Ma Taylor, Dorothy "Granny" Harris, Don Harris, Louise Hasty, Sam Hasty Sr., Annie White, Donovan Hasty, Jocelyn Hasty, Josie Lamberth, Marsherri French, Maurice white, Calandra Lidell, Michael Morino, Gregory O'bryant, Nick Colbert, Andre Johnson, Charlotte Patterson, Patrice Brown, Mike Brown, Chandra Patterson, Stacy Patterson, Mike Hasty, Demara Hasty, Beverly Holley, Bruce Holley, Andre Holley, Sam Hasty, Arlene Hasty, Joclyn Ross, Barbara Burns, Christine Taylor, Kesha Davis, Tracy Harris, Ashley Ingram, Renee Kinney, Mark Kinney, Marquita Kinney, Robert Hasty, Arnita Hasty, Angie Hasty, Larry Hasty, Renita Mcallister, Ryan Hasty, Kayla Hasty, Keith Mcallister, Marquan Williams, Jawan Williams, Kenny Hasty, Anthony Taylor, Sho, Dante Henley, Keith Henley, Scoob White, Ty Robinson, Khaleel Riley, Jordan Harris, Brittany Harris, Xavier Harris, Shantel Harris, Tanya Jonson, Shay Bradford, Cristal Harris, Nicky Harris, Porche O'Bryant, Dale Starks, Pat Starks, Gari Horn, Jan Howard, Tavarious Everson, Deabro Smith,

Tera Howard, Dante Berryhill, Mike Berryhill, Steve Berryhill, Emanual "Punkin'" Howard, Dre Berryhill, Joanne Berryhill, T'asia Brown, Janay Curtis, Tahj Kitt, Justin Starks, and Kenny Howard.

I want to give a special shout-out to my G street Chronicles family for believing in me and my work: George Hudson, Shawna A., Sabrina Eubanks, Cole Hart, India, Said Salaam, Mz. Robinson, Pinkey, V. Brown, and Tnicyo! We working over here, Jooooooooooooe!

I also want to give special thanks to all my friends and supporters: Norma Vandemark, Sandy Sims, Carla Towns, Lisa Perry, Nicole Farmer, Treasure Blue, K'wan Foye, Charolette Foye, Envy Red, Queen Brown, Kisha Green, Kai Storm, Tiffany Dean, Natisha Garrett, I'Kia Nicole, Monica Forbes, Yvette Hill, Nosha Peterson, Anissa Smith, D. Ladd, Cleopatra Isaac, Chakita Gordon, Michelle Thomas, Kylynn Aviles, Amanda Watson, Ellen Samuels, Shani Fenderson, Chunky Thickums, Shemika Jones, Tiffany Herrigan, Sabrina Hayes, Monique Reed, Jacqueline Harris, Che'Dolla Jenkins , Shantalle Brown, Adrenna Shipman, Helena Harris, Zaneta Powell, Chyta Curry, Dama Cargle, Pansy Jones, Terry Wroten, Coco Mixon, Lashawone Powell, Tiffany Hills, Rosalyn Reed, Twana Spencer, Brittani King, Mary Green, Melissa Haddix, Jacole Laryea, Yvonne Everette, Eyone Williams, Tomika Robinson, Nika Michelle, Lisa Greenleaf, Kayla Scurlock, Angela Day, Erica Jones, Ray Barlow, Secdka Cystrunk, Kena Cobb, James Terry, Qumeshia Thomas, Marina Johnson, Tajuana Williams, Kay Brown, Mark Jones, Tracy Jenkins, Nicosha Liddell, Linda Williams, Tamon Johnson, Cushenka Cunningham, Gail Jones, Heather Porch, Shaketa Jones, Alicia Campbell, Mary Lewis, Matt Brown, Tre- O, Abril Hall, Demeka Thompson, Kim Benjamin, Judon Hall, DJ Gold, Rickita Vaden, Michael Keon, Tyesha Banks, Erica Martinez, Ebony Vaughn, Lisa Colbert, Kjuana Brooks, Shikira Hoy, Shoney K., Julia Press Simmons, India Smith, Rahsaan Carr, Kamile Gardner, Camille Lamb, Geraldine

Grady, Sheffered Mclean, Kelly Dorsey, Josie Jo, Shaundus Johnson, Eugenia Parker, Tiffany Williams, Ms. Bossladii Daniels, Brandy Mays, Juanesia Walker, Sandy Gooden, Tiafrica Lucas, Latoya Knoll, Tamika Holt, Michelle Rawls, DC Book Diva, TLJ Bookstore, Cartel Bookstore, Black and Nobel, Hood Bookstore, Delonya Conyers, Oosa Book Club, Michael Siemens, Tasha Parker, Dionne Kilpatrick, Kesha West, Sherene Vaughn, Lawanda Tanner, Wesley Hanna, Staff O' Bryant, Boshae Myers, Lesa Jones, Taneisha Stackhouse, Kitty Johnson, Anita Buttercup, Monica Phelps, Latosha Williams, Fred Flemming, Tasha Ladd, Cris Foster, Angela Kidd, D-Ball, Missy Randolph, Charlana Jackson, Smokey da Bandit, Byron Ferguson, Antony Love, Willi D., Eric Green, Candy Johnson, Rufus Duncan, Jermaine Turner, Ralph Linder, Latonya Alex, Yvonne Stovall, Shawn Fisher, Josh Alex, Sadeka Young, Larry Lynch, Robert Hopson, Charles Ramsey, Larry Mackins, Trell Mackins, Bo, Sabrina Lynch, Randa Pink, Leo Presley, Sabrina West, Terrance Perry, Cherri Broughton, Duv Ent, Victoria Butler, Takina Garland, Kenny Keys, the North Chicago Warhawks, Latasha Mckelvy, Fawn Matthews, Shelmar Mays, Shawn Stackhouse, Calvin Myers, Mark Miller, Poky, Lasone Moment, Brittany Givens, Kevin Strawder, Carl Dumas, Daphne Kilpatrick, Cedrick Lee, Michael Bone, Blockboy Calvin, Shannele Mc Bride, Markeisha Nairn, Marcus Rogers, Yarbia Coleman, Pricilla Brown, Natoya Taylor, Black and Faithful Brothers and Sisters Book Club, Black Pearl, Nook Readers Book Club, Rasheed Carter, OTB Pro, Mike Calvert, AC, Jack D., Curtis Pride, Gucci, Crissie Friar, Kim Edwards, Johns Liquor, Legal Dope Radio, B.M.G, Brandie Davis, Jesse Florez, Sherry Phillips, Ashley Whitley, Daisha Laboria, Ladonna Humes, Kamilah Little, Ketra Cobb, Lasonette Bradlely, Turquoise, Artisa Hall, Anton Campbell, Jay Junya, Rashon Edwards, Shirl Palmer, Amber Johnson, Tianna Widermyre, Cristina Keaton, Gabriel Dotson, Kathy Clayborne, Shana Glenn, Shayla Mc CLain, Melissa Tyler, Corn Corleon, Mau, Kristy Bluitt, Barbara Young,

Keno Young, Andre Warship, Dante Brooks, Shima Davis, Shan Gradney, Rashid Pool, Tanika McGill, Darlina Bosley, Sikira Hoy, Martina Beasley, Twin Tower Ent, Franks be Jukin, Big Eds Bar b que, Denise Downs, Detrick Adams, Charlene Miller, Winston Wade, Shannon Shaw, Casaundra Alex, Tamika Johnson, Natasha Parks, Candis Ridgeway, Cassondra Hanna, Jasmine Johnson, Erika Romeo, Swan Marshall, Keilen Smith, Kelle Riley, Karen Cummings, Lisa Olan, Torcivia Daniels, Step the Producer, Music Son, North Chicag Liqour, IGA Liquors, Bionce Foxx, Blocklife Books, Kush and Koolaid Ent, UDG Records, Dirty Church Socks, Simone Bridges, Get em Girls Ent, Lakisha Lowe, Tiffany Tabb, 28 Gram Ent, Chantaye Sanders, Erica Agee, Tisheila Early, Explicit Ent, Block Boy City Ent, Belvidere Blues, Larry Hailey, Quin Johnson, Natasha Banks, Denise Houston, Kim Moore, Denisha McCauley, Doreen Johnson, Michael Pillips, Byron Craig, Fat How, Kill Will, Sameia Charity, Ryan Duncan, Keira Keys, Tiffany Keys, Brandon Brooks, Tanesha Reid, Mirrlees Duggins, Douglas Harris, Tanya McCarthy, Sexy, Déjà vu Book Lounge, Nicole Leflore, Deanna Bouie, Ernestine Brown, Racine Twon, Racine Shawn, Racine Goldie, Royal Morris, Andrea Rowland, Bryce, Ray Crockette, Keith Paige, Jimmie Jonson, Li'l jimmy, Serry Walker, Rell Johnson, Geno Adams, Greg Adams, Squeek D., Big Mook, BD Doug, Ced D., Sonny Stranger, Genoris Green, Tosha Golden, Tamara Craig, Patricia Jones, Joy Henderson, Ericka McCoy, Tonie Masie, Trayce Irvin, Li'l Pooh, Big Richardson, Cicely Tucker, Nicholas Kane, CeaseFire, DJ 262, Yasheca Johnson, A. Lux, Alexia Edmonds, Nate'le Harris, 21st Editing and Publishing, David Weaver, Mikie Da Grip, The Writer Formerlly Known as Mikeo, My Urban Book Club, Black e-Book Club, DJ Gatsby Book Club, Fun4damental Book Club, Kindle and Paperback Book Club, Urban Written, We Read Urban Fiction Book Club, and Word on the Street Publishing.

And finally, to all those who said I couldn't make it, Team Awsum working over here!

I dedicate this book to my fallen soldiers, Isaac Roland and Gregory "Gumpy" Colbert.

"Flight 377, I'm on an all-night flight!"

G STREET CHRONICLES
A NEW URBAN DYNASTY

WWW.GSTREETCHRONICLES.COM

PART I

BLOOD IN

WWW.GSTREETCHRONICLES.COM

PROLOGUE

G STREET CHRONICLES

A NEW URBAN DYNASTY

WWW.GSTREETCHRONICLES.COM

The highway was empty as the white Benz sped through the night air. The light drizzles of rain danced across the windshield as the sounds of the Clipse Grinding blasted through the speakers. They say female drivers drive faster than men; this was definitely one of those cases, as the woman driving the 2001 white Mercedes-Benz on the twenty-two-inch rims was pushing ninety in a sixty-five, as if she didn't care for the rules of the road. Unfortunately for her, it was the police she had just flown by, sitting there on the side of the road in their Chevy Suburban police truck. The officers quickly hit their lights and sirens and pulled out in hot pursuit. The officers were charged up, ready for a chase, and the K-9 sounded as if he was instigating them with each bark.

The driver of the Benz looked in the rearview and saw the flashing lights behind her. "Damn! Here goes these muthafuckas. I definitely don't have time for this tonight!" she said, thinking out loud. As bad as she wanted to ignore them, she knew it would only make matters worse, so she decided to pull over to the side and try and get the situation over with as quickly as possible.

The police pulled up behind her on the empty highway. The officers quickly jumped out and took their positions, following the proper procedures for a pull-over. The stocky, dark-haired white officer approached the driver side window while his blond partner took his position behind the car.

The window of the Benz came down, and the female driver quickly stuck out her hand, offering her license and insurance.

"Put your arm back in the vehicle, ma'am! Just sit back and relax!" he said. He now could see the driver. Black girls weren't his taste though. He actually despised them and their nigger boyfriends, but this black bitch had long, straight, jet-black hair and sexy brown eyes that actually caught his attention. He couldn't help but look down between her thick brown thighs, exposed under her black mini-skirt that didn't even hide the red lace panties she was wearing.

She knew what he was looking at, so she helped him out a little and adjusted herself so he could get a good look. Once she knew she had his full attention, she quickly snapped her legs together and pulled her skirt down. "Excuse me, Officer Pervert! The peep show cost!" she said, snapping at the officer.

"You black bitch! What'd you just say to me?" the officer asked, his face turning red as a fire truck from his embarrassment. He quickly unholstered his firearm and pointed at the lady driver as if he'd seen a gun, causing his partner to draw his weapon as well. "Get the fuck out the car, bitch!" he demanded as he grabbed the door handle with his left hand while holding his gun tightly in his right hand.

"Did I hit a nerve, Officer Pervert? I'm sorry. So you wanted a *free* show, huh?" she said. She laughed as she got out of the car.

The officer wasted no time grabbing her and throwing her up against the car as hard as he could.

"Pete, you want me to call this one in?" his partner yelled to him, but he was blinded by rage and almost didn't respond.

"Naw, partner. We gonna have some fun with this bitch!" He pulled her to the back of her car. "Put your fucking hands on the car and spread your legs!"

She gave no resistance as he began his pat-down.

He began by grabbing her breasts and squeezing them as he aggressively rubbed down her body till his hands were in between her thighs. His fingers found their way into her panties; to his surprise and delight, she was soaked. "Yeah, bitch, I knew you were a fucking slut. All you black bitches are!" he hissed in her ear as his fingers continued exploring her wetness.

His partner had now come close and began touching her as well. They were ready to fuck her right there on the back of the car, and clearly, the thought of treating a black female like a whore turned them on.

"Is this your name on your plates, bitch?" Pete asked, grabbing her by her long hair and not giving her a chance to answer. "Tish, huh? Partner, you every fucked anybody named Tish before?"

"Hell naw!"

"Me neither. I guess tonight's our lucky night. Cuff this bitch while I check the car."

"Peter the pervert! Peter the pervert!" Tish chanted as he walked away and began searching her car.

He reached under the seat and felt the cold steel of a gun. He quickly grabbed it. His adrenalin was now pumping, and he didn't even realize the chanting had stopped. As he rose from the car, looking back toward the female driver and his partner, he couldn't believe what he saw. Nobody was there! He pulled his gun back out, crouched down, and made his way toward the back of the car. The K-9 in the car was going crazy, barking in the distance. Peter's approach was slow, as the drizzling rain had turned into snowflakes. "Partner!" he yelled.

No response.

He stopped at the back end of the car, still crouched down and holding his gun tightly. As he glanced downward, he saw a long stream of blood rolling across the ground in front of him. He jumped from behind the car, and his eyes grew as wide as silver dollars. There, beneath his feet, was his partner, handcuffed, with a blood-gushing gash going from ear to ear. Pete's mind was lost. His first thought was to call it in, but he froze up while his partner chocked on his own blood. He did his best to help his partner, trying to stop the blood from shooting out his neck, but it was no good. A moment later, his partner's eyes rolled back in his head, and he died, right there in the falling snow. Pete couldn't believe what was happening and was almost in shock, but he quickly snapped back to reality when the chant began again.

"Peter the pervert! Peter the pervert!"

He started shooting, gripping his gun with his blood-covered hands, but he didn't know where the voice was coming from; his anger was blinding him. He unloaded his whole clip into the darkness of the night, not hitting anybody. While he quickly reloaded, the K-9 went crazy, barking and whining to be freed so he could get his teeth into the action. *This black bitch wanna play? We can play,* Pete thought to himself as he made his way back toward his truck. His footsteps ended abruptly at the sound of the gunfire that came from the other side of his car. One bullet buzzed by just inches from his head, causing him to hit the ground to escape the blast. Unfortunately, the K-9 wasn't as lucky; two bullets ripped through the back of the police car and right into the dog's head, sending its brains splashing all over the back window. The officer could hear the whimpers of his dog, but there was nothing he could do at that point but call it in and hope for backup. He quickly grabbed his radio on his shoulder and began speaking. "Officers down! Officers down!" he yelled into his radio to dispatch. "Backup requested! Officer down! I repeat, office—" But he didn't have a chance to repeat, for his hand exploded at the wrist from a bullet that seemed to come out of nowhere.

"This is dispatch. Officer, what's your location? Over."

The officer wanted to respond, but all he could do was scream with pain and look at all the blood coming from where his hand use to be. "You black bitch! Look what you did to me!" he yelled.

There was only laughter in response.

He was lying three feet from his gun, which was by the front tire of the police car; he was beyond pain, and vengeance was now his fuel as he began crawling toward his gun with blood running from his wound. Dispatch continued to talk through the radio, but he didn't care. He grabbed the gun with his only hand. "Yeah, bitch, you wanna play rough, huh? I'm going to kill you and fuck your dead body!" he yelled as he began making his way to his knees, leaning up against the police car driver side door. He took his time peeking through the windows of the car to look for his target, but he didn't see anything. "Here, kitty, kitty! Come here and let me fuck you like the nasty black cunt you are!" he taunted.

"Peter!"

The response made his heart drop out of his body, because the words were coming from the *top* of the car! He slowly looked up and there she was, standing on top of the car, right over his head, aiming his partner's gun down at him! "Please! I got a family!" he began pleading.

But she just smiled as she pulled her skirt up with one hand and kept aim with the other .

The officer didn't know what to do or say as she put her hand in her panties and began playing with her pussy.

"What's wrong, Peter the pervert? You wanted to play, didn't you?" she said as she stuck her fingers inside her pussy and began slowly sliding them in and out, playing in her wetness and moaning as she continued talking. "Mmm... Don't you wanna play anymore, Peter Pervert?"

He didn't respond. He was waiting on his chance to get a shot off, and he saw it coming as he watched her body shake and her eyes close as if she were reaching a climax. Now was the time. He quickly began raising his gun toward the female, whose eyes were now closed, but he never got a chance.

Without even opening her eyes, she squeezed the trigger, sending a bullet exploding out the barrel of the gun and smashing right through the middle of his forehead, making a doggy flap out the back of his head. "OOOOOOOOOOOOOh shit!" she screamed with pleasure as cum ran all down her legs. Within minutes, she was back in her car. She was running late for her dinner date with death; the police and their dog were just appetizers. She put her Benz in gear and pulled away from the bloody scene, speeding off into the night.

As she drove into the darkness, she couldn't help but look at her reflection in the review mirror. Her deep brown eyes had such a story to tell. For the first time in her life, she knew exactly who she was, as her life, up till that moment, flipped through her mind like the pages of a book.

WWW.GSTREETCHRONICLES.COM

CHAPTER ONE

Blood Red

WWW.GSTREETCHRONICLES.COM

It was January 9, 1991. Even though New Year's had been over for a week, the short, brown-skinned lady everybody called Rose had kept the party going all week, and even though it was Sunday, her get-together was in full swing. Clouds of cigarette and marijuana smoke filled the air over the kitchen table, which was now serving as a card table. That table was covered with money and glasses of Crown Royal, and at the end of the table was Rose, with about $3,000 in cash in front of her.

Larry, Rose's boyfriend for the week, was sitting right behind her, nursing a drink and counting Rose's money. Rose kept a revolving door of niggas. Her five-three frame, silky brown skin, and hips that hung off the side of her chair kept dudes coming around like clockwork—not to mention she kept more money than them and had no problem spending it.

Larry was an up-and-coming pimp, and he had been working on Rose all week. With his long, silky black hair and slick mouthpiece, it was almost impossible to deny him. As he sat his six-two frame back in his chair, nursing his Crown Royal, he watched Rose's winnings and thought of a plan. Even though Rose was definitely a prize to have on his team, the prize he really wanted was her fourteen-year-old daughter Latisha. His eyes had been watching her all week like a predator looking for his prey.

Latisha didn't look like the average fourteen-year-old. She had a smooth, light caramel complexion, hypnotizing brown eyes, and hips like a grown woman. That, combined with the fact that she'd been wearing a bra since she was twelve, meant her body was perfect.

Larry had seen many females in his lifetime, but he had never seen one as pretty as Latisha, and he knew if he had her on his team she would make him rich. Larry had been lying up with Rose all week, waiting on his moment to strike, and as he looked around at the six drunken people in the kitchen playing poker, he knew there was no time like the present, especially since he could feel his dick getting hard just thinking about what he was about to do to her. Within seconds, he had excused himself to the bathroom, but instead of going to the bathroom, he was now standing at Latisha's bedroom door.

The sleeping Latisha was lying in the bed in her t-shirt and panties when the light from the hallway light flashed across her face, making her open her eyes to see what was going on. Her focus was still blurry, but she could see someone coming at her fast.

Before she could move or say a word, Larry was on top of her with his right hand over her mouth and his left hand holding a straight razor to her face. "Bitch, if you make a noise, I'll slit your fucking throat!" Larry said as he removed his hand from the frightened girl's face and used it to pull out his erect dick.

The tears ran down her face from the pain of his penetration. She was a virgin, and he tore her wide open.

Larry had no choice but to put his hand back over her mouth to stop her from screaming as he tried to push his way all the way in. He was about to start talking to her, but her tightness and his excitement made him bust his load in her, and the rest leaked out on her bloody panties. Larry wasted no time pulling his pants up as he watched the girl cry.

Latisha felt like she was paralyzed; she was scared to move.

Then Larry pulled a $100 bill from his pocket and shoved it in her mouth. "You belong to me now, bitch. If you tell anybody about tonight, I'm gonna kill you and your mother!" Larry said before he crept out of the room.

* * *

When the morning came, Latisha was in the shower at 5 a.m. in the hottest water she could take. The scalding-hot water ran down her body, mixed in with the salty tears that ran from her eyes, as she scrubbed and scrubbed her body so she could stop feeling dirty. She quickly got dressed and was out the door, doing her best to avoid Rose and Larry.

Even though it was the first day back from winter break,

the day when kids loved to go back to school to show off what they got for Christmas, Latisha never went into the building. Instead, she walked to the park and sat on the swing. She didn't swing; she just sat there crying into her hands until she was startled by approaching footsteps and a voice she would never forget.

"Are you all right?" the deep, grimy voice asked.

"I'm fine," Latisha said, looking up at the six-four, 236-pound, light-skinned man with six thick braids going to the back and twelve gold trims covering his front teeth.

"I mean, you're over here crying…all alone."

"Who are you, some kind of guardian angel or something? What, you just walk around all day looking for crying females? If it will make you leave me alone, I'll tell you what's wrong with me. I got raped, okay? Happy now?" She couldn't even hold her head up, for she was weighed down by her shame.

"Latisha, who raped you?" the man demanded.

"How do you know my name?" she replied in a sobbing voice as she looked back up and saw the fury in the man's eyes.

"Who was he!?" was all the man said.

At that time, she asked no more questions. "My mom's boyfriend Larry."

"Where is he at right now?" the man asked.

"Probably at the house still asleep, but…but I'm not supposed to tell anybody, or else he's going to kill me and my mom!" Latisha said with a scared look on her face.

"Let's go. It's time we had a few words with this Larry," replied the man.

Even though he was a stranger to her, Latisha stood up and followed the man to his all-black '69 two-door Cutlass. There was something about the man that made her feel safe, *But it's definitely not those gold trims on his teeth*, she thought to herself as the Cutlass sped down the road on its way to her house.

Rose had already left for work. Latisha wasted no time letting the man in her house and pointing him toward the bedroom where Larry was.

Larry was in bed, sound asleep in his wife-beater and some red silk boxers, when the stranger grabbed him out of the bed by his neck. Larry instantly woke up, feeling a grip around his neck like a vice. He was overpowered by the man's strength and was dragged to the living room, kicking and trying to scream. Once the stranger let go of him, he found himself sitting in the middle of the floor, looking like he wanted to kill somebody. "This is my house mu'fucka! You best get the fuck ou—" But Larry never got to finish his sentence before he found himself looking down the barrel of a .357 Python.

"Now that I've got your attention, you piece of shit, the best advice I can give you is that you shut the fuck up and listen. Out of all the females in the world, you chose this one to put your filthy hands on," the stranger said.

"I…I…I would never…I wouldn't do that!" Larry said in a pleading voice, looking at Latisha, who was standing behind her guardian angel with tears of anger coming down her face, looking at the man who had violated her.

"If you say one more fucking word, I'll kill you dead, bitch. I can't believe you put your hands on my niece," the stranger said, with his trigger finger trembling from wanting to squeeze it so badly. "It's all right. Your Uncle Red isn't going to let nothing else happen to you, baby. I promise." Red knew with his brother going to prison, it was his job to look after Latisha, and there he was passing the gun to his niece.

Latisha was nervous, but she held the massive .357.

'That's it. Hold it with both hands, "Red said, guiding her.

"Latisha, I was drunk. I'll never touch you again, I promise. I made a…a mistake!" pleaded Larry.

"You fucking right you made a mistake," Latisha replied as she squeezed the trigger, letting off a sound like an explosion, sending a bullet right through the man's eye and out the back of his head.

Red softly grabbed the gun.

Latisha turned around, whispering, "Are you really my uncle?"

"Yes, baby, and everything is going to be all right. But we have to leave here and never come back."

"What about my mom?" asked Latisha.

"She's not your mom, Latisha, and I promise I'll explain everything to you in a minute. Right now I need you to go get your stuff and let me take care of Larry," Red replied.

Latisha's mind was racing as she ran in her room and packed as fast as she could. Within five minutes, she emerged out of her room, ready to ask a million questions, but she never got to open her mouth.

Red started talking while he cleaned Larry's blood off the floor. "Your real parents' names are Tyler and Debra Scott, also known as King and Queen. Rose is your mother's sister, and I'm your father's older brother. Oh yeah...you got two little brothers too. They twins," he said, looking up at his niece, who was standing there looking confused. "I know all this is a little confusing right now. Just know you were put here for your protection and not because you're not loved. We're from a rare bloodline, baby girl!" Red said. He could definitely tell she had their blood pumping through her, since the fourteen-year-old female had just blown a man's brains all over the floor and was now acting like nothing had even happened.

Latisha had never seen anybody clean up a dead body before, but by the way her uncle moved, she could tell he'd done it many times before. Within ten twenty minutes, Red had cleaned everything up, wrapped Larry in a rug, put him in the trunk, and they were on the road. As they drove, headed to God-knew-where, Latisha couldn't believe she had killed a man, but she had no remorse. All she left behind was a letter to Rose: "Dear Aunt Rose: I'm leaving and never coming back. Don't try to find me because you won't be able to. Just know I'm safe now. It's time for me to move on and be the princess I'm supposed to be. Love,

Princess Tisha."

* * *

As Red drove, he knew life was about to change. It had started a couple of weeks earlier, on Christmas, when his brother was arrested for killing a police officer. Red hated that his brother was locked up, but his brother had already warned him it was going to happen. Red admired his little brother when it came to getting money, but when it came to strategy, his brother always saw ten steps ahead and planned twenty. So, when Red got the phone call telling him his brother was locked up, he knew exactly what to do. Only one person outside of Rose, King, and Queen knew Latisha existed, and that was the one who'd set his brother up.

Red couldn't help but smile thinking about how many ways he could kill Benny. Benny had been best friends with his brother since they were kids. The three of them had had the dope game on lock since Red and King had killed the city's drug lord, Big Tony, back in the day. Even though they had more money than a black man could even imagine, Benny was always jealous of King because King had all the connects and made the most money, and people worshipped him like a real king. Benny knew King was far too powerful so he just played his role till the opportunity arose for him to take the king out. Red and King both knew Benny was going to sell King out, especially when King told him he was quitting the dope game and was going to stop all the drugs from coming into the 'hood. Benny couldn't believe what King was saying and then, to put the icing on the cake, King told Benny he had the recipe for a drug that would take over the white communities across the United States. Red told King not to tell Benny about that, but all King said to his warning was, "You can show someone your cards, but they still can't play them for you. Dropping a drug this powerful right now is not going to work. This has to be a perfectly calculated plan. If Benny runs and tells Agent Fellows like I think he gon' do, we've already completed the first step in our plan."

Red was confused and wondered why they didn't just kill everybody and take over.

King quickly continued, knowing his brother too well. "Big bro, let me break it down like this…we fighting for the heavyweight championship, and the boxer we fighting for the belt we get to spar against all the way up until the day of the fight. By the time the fight come, I'm going to know they every move. We just jabbing right now, learning they defense. You dig?" said King, swinging a right hook at Red.

Red put his guard up quickly but still caught a blow under the chin.

"See, nigga, all these years, and you still hold your guard too high." King finished, laughing as Red attempted to hit him back.

That's how they'd played they whole life. Red loved his little brother, and he was the only one in the world who could get a lick off on him without dying. Even though King was playing, Red got his message loud and clear. That was the last conversation Red got to have with his brother King, because just what they thought Benny was going to do, he did.

* * *

Red had been watching Latisha for a couple days; he knew they would send a hit team to kill her, especially since they didn't get the secret drug they were looking for when King killed the police officer. If Larry wouldn't have pulled that bullshit with his niece, Red could've waited till the hit squad was sent and killed them all. *But it is what it is,* he thought to himself, looking over at his niece, who had fallen asleep in the passenger seat. No matter the case, she was his responsibility now. He had already let somebody hurt her once, and there definitely wouldn't be a second time.

Red couldn't do anything but shake his head, disappointed in himself – especially since he owed King his life. That was something he could never forget, even though it happened fourteen years ago.

* * *

The powder cocaine era was at its peak, and King and Red had they hands in all of it. Even though the Italian mafia was against selling drugs at the beginning, they couldn't even pass up all that money. They wasted no time becoming the number one supplier and King's main connect. Everything was going smooth as could be, until the Colombians wanted to take over as the new suppliers. The war was instantly on. The Colombians and the Italians turned the streets into rivers of blood, and the stench of death filled the night air. In just two weeks, thirty bodies had turned up: ten Italians and twenty Colombians. There were other bodies that hadn't turned up, or else they were found with no heads, arms, or legs, so it was impossible to identify what side they were on. Even though the Colombians seemed to be losing the war, they showed no sign of letting up; if they couldn't take the Italians down directly, they would attack those who dealt with them. On the top of that list were King and Red.

It was 3 a.m. when King and Red pulled in front of Red's house. They had just left the club, where they'd celebrated the purchase they'd just made. It's one thing to buy a house, but when you buy the housing project you grew up in, that's definitely means for a celebration. King was still drinking Crown Royal straight out the bottle. He had the pretty purple velvet Crown Royal bag with the gold drawstrings pulled down just enough to sip out of. They were fucked up as they sat in the car, looking like twins from their features to their all-black outfits.

Red took his time getting out of King's Jaguar taking an extra couple steps as he stood up.

"I'll get at you tomorrow, bro. Let me get home to Deb. She might have that baby any moment now," King said, proud that he was about to be a father for the first time.

"Plus, it's cold, nigga! Close the door!"

"Fuck you, nigga…and this door!" Red replied, causing them to laugh as he closed the door.

King sped off from the curb like a bat out of hell.

An all-black Benz riding by slow caught Red's attention, causing him to turn around. He couldn't see the driver, but he made direct eye contact with a dark-haired man in the back of the car who looked like he was smiling as the car kept rolling by. The incident made Red reach for his gun. "Damn! I forgot my pistol in the car!" he said, thinking out loud, as he proceeded toward his big white house. "Fuck it. I'll just get that shit in the morning." He put his key in the door and turned it. Until he opened the door to a pitch-black crib, he hadn't noticed that his Rottweilers weren't barking. As he closed the door behind him, he was struck on the side of his head with something hard, leaving him unconscious from the blow.

* * *

As King turned the first couple corners, heading home, he quickly saw an all-black Ford Bronco following him. At first he thought he was just being paranoid, but when there was no such thing as paranoid in a life like his, and that caused him to open his middle console to get his gun out. As he looked over to grab his .44 Bulldog revolver, he saw the handle of Red's .357 stuffed in the side of the passenger seat. King was going to play it smooth at first, but he had to get back to his brother. As King approached the stop sign, he saw that the black truck had picked up speed. King griped his pistol tightly, knowing someone was going to die that night.

* * *

The screams of his wife and the cold steel of a shotgun pressed to his head brought Red back to consciousness. The once dark house was now full of light and three armed Colombians. One was holding the shotgun, pointed at Red as he sat on the couch, and one was holding a .45 to the head of Red's light-skinned wife Stacy, who was on her knees. The one who looked to be in charge was walking back and forth, holding Red's ten-month-old baby daughter Simone with one hand and his blue steel .45 automatic in the other. As he looked at his wife's tears running down her face, Red knew he had to be cool to get them out of it, but no sooner than the thought came to his mind, the Colombian squeezed the trigger, sending Stacy brains across the living room floor.

"One down, two to go," the slick-haired Columbian man said in his expensive suit as he held Red's daughter, rubbing the barrel of the .45 across the baby's face, like he was soothing her fears from the sound of the gun going off.

* * *

King sat at the stop sign, watching and waiting as the truck approached fast. When it was less than a half-block away, King threw the Jag in reverse and slammed the pedal to the floor. The power of the Jag was undeniable, even going in reverse, and the tires gripped into the concrete like they had claws. The driver of the Bronco slammed on the brakes, but it was already too late to avoid the back of the Jaguar as it came smashing into the front of the truck.

The Jaguar took the worst of the collision, but the drivers of the truck should have put their seatbelts on. The mouth of the Colombian was smashed open on the steering wheel. His front teeth were all gone, and the blood poured from his mouth as he fumbled around for the MAC-10 machine gun he'd had on his lap before the accident. Even though he was disorientated, he spotted it lying on the floor down by the gas pedal, and he quickly tried to grab it. His actions were stopped abruptly as his car door flew open and he was grabbed by the back of his hair.

Before the Colombian could react, King had snatched him up by the man's long ponytail. King wasted no time in pushing his pistol into the man's bloody mouth and pulling the trigger, sending blood and brain matter splashing all over the passenger, who was struggling to move; the crash had broken both of his legs. The passenger just put his hands up in a surrendering motion as he looked at King, who standing there with blood splattered across his light-skinned face. King just grinned at him, showing his gold teeth, then raised his pistol once again and squeezed it, sending a bullet right through the man's hand that he was holding up and landing in the man's neck. The blood squirted all over the inside of the truck as the man tried his best to hold on to the gaping hole that was now in his neck. King laughed as he squeezed the .44 Bulldog two more times, giving the man two more slugs to the chest and putting him out of his misery. Within seconds, King was back in the wrecked Jaguar, on his way back to Red.

* * *

Red had been in a lot of situations before, but none quite this. *There's no point in asking these muthafuckas what they want*, Red thought to himself as he sat on the couch. He already knew they were going to kill his whole family, him included.

The Colombian with the suit on finally put the baby down on the floor right next to what was left of her mother. The baby crawled through her mother's blood and pieces of her skull that were scattered everywhere, unaware that anything was wrong.

Red had seen enough. It was time to make a move, even if it got him killed. He noticed that the man with the shotgun on him was looking at the baby, and he knew he could tackle the one who had shot his wife, since he was the closest, but just as he got ready to make his move, the suit squeezed the trigger of his gun two times, shooting the baby. Red's heart dropped out his body, and he froze, but then he heard a familiar sound coming from behind him that brought him back into focus. It was the *pitter-patter* of his three-year-old son No'fere, who'd been hiding in the living room closet the whole time. The gunman's attention was quickly drawn toward the little boy, and Red wasted no time jumping into action. The gunman who'd killed his wife never even saw the train with no brakes, that train called Red, coming full speed at him. Red hit him with so much force that the man was asleep before he was driven into the wall, shaking the house.

As the other two gunman turned to take aim at Red, the glass sliding doors in the living room seemed to explode from the bullets of the .44 Bulldog and the .357 Python King was wielding in both hands. The man in the suit caught a bullet from the .357 high in his shoulder, spinning him around and dropping him to the floor. The shotgun-toting Colombian dodged two bullets that landed in the wall behind his head, and he quickly returned fire, making King hit the floor.

The little boy stood in the middle of the floor, paralyzed with fear, as the man turned the shotgun toward him. Red moved without thinking as the man cocked the shotgun, ready to kill his son. Red was over the couch within seconds and dove for his son as the shotgun went off. King felt like life was going in slow motion as he watched the buck shots from the shotgun knock Red out of the air, causing him to fall on top of No'fere.

King was blind with rage. He lifted both guns while he ran toward the man with the shotgun, pulling both triggers simultaneously. The Colombian with the shotgun tried to turn back toward King, but he never had a chance. He took a .44 bullet in his cheek that came out the back of his head, followed by two slugs slamming into his chest, sending him into the wall and leaving blood smears as he slid down to the ground breathless. The man with the suit was lying on the floor by the front door, trying to crawl toward his gun three feet away, feeling the burn from his gunshot wound with each movement. He was stopped in his tracks by King, who was now standing over him holding both guns at his side. King looked over at his sister-in-law and his niece in a puddle of their own blood. The wounded Colombian sat up, giving up his struggle to get to the gun; he knew it was over for him. King raised the guns slowly, as the man spoke.

"Fuck you and your family!" he said, spitting on the floor like he was spitting on their graves.

King began to squeeze the triggers, but breathing coming from right behind him startled him, causing him to turn around. King found himself looking into the eyes of a beast with no soul, only rage. King didn't speak; he just put his guns back to his side and stepped aside. King could see that Red had been shot badly in his back, as his black t-shirt looked like it was soaking wet as the blood dripped from the bottom of it onto the floor. Red's anger and hurt was his fuel as he cocked the shotgun he had picked up off the floor and took aim at the Colombian.

The Colombian's eyes grew big as he saw a dead man aiming the shotgun at his head.

"Fuck you!" Red said, pulling the trigger. The close

range of the shotgun left the man headless. Red then turned toward his wife and daughter, lying there lifeless, and fell unconscious to the floor in a puddle of their blood.

* * *

Red had been unconscious for three days, and the last thing he remembered was seeing an older black man with circle-lens glasses standing over him, pulling buck shots out of his back and dropping them in a little metal bowl that was on a table next to the man. He didn't know if it was the medication or the thought of losing his whole family that had him feeling no pain inside or out, but whatever the case, numbness filled his body from head to toe. As he opened his eyes for the first time in several days, he didn't know if he was dead or alive. He'd always heard that when you die, you walk into a bright light, and that was all he could see since his vision was still blurry. He could hear voices in the distance, but he couldn't make the words out.

Then a voice came from over him, snapping him into focus. "Damn, Red. How long you gon' sleep?" King asked, standing over his brother, who was lying on his stomach on an old hospital bed.

Red had an IV in his arm and bandages covering his back. Lucky for him, he'd only taken half the blast from the shotgun, or else he definitely would have been dead.

"Red, wake your ass up, before I slap you on your back," King said, lifting his hand like he was going to carry out his threat.

"Nigga, don't make me fuck you up!" Red murmured, trying not to laugh at his little brother.

"Nigga, you been in here asleep for three days with a graze wound!" King said, making light of the situation.

"Don't make me laugh. This shit hurt, nigga," Red replied, feeling the pain in his back from trying not to laugh. *The only pain I can't stop is seeing my family slaughtered in front of me,* he thought to himself. He was so caught up in the thought he almost didn't hear King talking to him.

"Red? Red!" King said, trying to get Red's attention as he bent down to reach for something. "Somebody wants to say hi!" King said, now holding Red's son No'fere in his arms, unharmed. King couldn't even imagine the pain his brother was going through. His own daughter, Latisha, had been born the same night when Red had lost his wife and daughter, and that made King instantly put her in hiding.

"How's the patient doing?" asked the Professor, a little black man in wire-framed glasses, taking a sip from his flask.

"I'm good. Thanks for saving me, Doc!" Red replied, even though he knew he was still hurt.

The Professor was known as the doctor to the criminals, and he was damn good at what he did. With a war going on, his place might as well have had a revolving door, but when your name is King, shop is closed. Red would be the only patient until he got better. The Professor didn't care. King paid top dollar, and he always listened to his stories about a drug he could make that would take over the world. Red would've never guessed that fourteen years later, it would be that very drug that would send King to jail.

* * *

Red thoughts were broken by the sound of Latisha waking up after a two-hour nap as Red drove in to the City of Vision.

"Where are we, Unc?" Latisha asked, looking out the window into the unfamiliar city.

"Welcome to the jungle, baby girl!" Red replied. Latisha was like having a second chance to have a daughter, and he wasn't gone to fail again.

CHAPTER TWO

Junior

Nine Years Later

It was five degrees below zero in the vacant uptown apartment as the hooded individual watched from the window, looking through his night-vision goggles at the fancy Waltz Hotel across the street. He had spotted his target over an hour earlier, followed by seven bodyguards and two heavily armed U.S. marshals. It looked like an easy hit, for the average hit man, but that what it was made to look like. The whole scene was a hoax, because down the street two blocks away, two black Suburbans were parked. Those Suburbans contained eight more goons, ready to come and kill at the drop of a dime. Inside the hotel were two more marshals, one posing as a doorman and another posing as a desk clerk – not to mention the eight more in the penthouse suite and the four crooked feds in the apartment below the hooded individual, doing surveillance.

The target's name was Juan Carlos, also known as Junior. He was the son of Colombian cartel boss Juan Carlos, El Capitan, the most feared drug lord in Colombia. Junior handled the cartel's business in the United States, and he was the voice for his father, who hadn't stepped foot in the States in twenty years. Junior's father knew it wasn't safe for him or his son to be there as much as Junior was, but Junior was ruthless, hard-headed, and loved to party. So, he visited twice a month and always stayed for three days at a time. He met his under boss, Miguel (aka Spider) to make sure the shipment and the money was right, and then they partied like rock stars. He was gone just like clockwork. Even though he followed an obvious pattern, that routine was well calculated, and it had been his key to survival over the years. There'd been well over twenty failed attempts on his life, and with a one million-dollar dead and a two million-dollar alive price on the heads of him and his father, somebody was always gunning for him. Junior made sure he stuck to his strict routine. The only thing that ever changed were the females he partied with. That was number one on his list; even though he hated to admit it, even he knew his weakness was females. Number two on his list was his timing. He came in anytime, and his fast departures made it hard for a hit man to set up on him; by the time they got the intel on where he was in order to kill him, it was already too late, and he was gone like yesterday till the next time. He had maintained this pattern for the last five years. Unfortunately for Junior, this was his eighth day in the city.

The hooded man couldn't do anything but smile, seeing the glare from his gold teeth in his reflection in the window he was looking out of. *Game time,* the hooded man thought to himself as he turned from the window and went for his long black case on the floor. "Death is promised!" he found himself saying, thinking out loud as he knelt down to open the latches on the black case, getting ready to set up for the night's festivities.

Junior paced the floor in his room in his luxury five-bedroom penthouse. The ladies he was going to party with that night hadn't arrived yet. *With the week I've had, I need to release some steam,* thought the five-nine, dark-haired Colombian, dressed like Tony Montana. He quickly walked over to his desk, where he had an ounce of raw cocaine. Federal marshals were in the next room, but Junior didn't care, and neither did they. The marshals were enjoying the parties and all the amenities that came along with watching a billionaire's son. Junior pulled out his rolled-up $100 bill from his pocket and stuck it in the cocaine, then put his nostril to the other end and took a deep sniff. The numbness filled his face as his last week flashed through his mind.

* * *

It had been a routine trip for Junior. He'd met Spider in the Columbians' warehouse. The sound of money counters filled the air, mixed in with the forklifts moving pallets of cocaine from the semi. It took a mere twenty minutes for them to weigh in 999 kilos of 100 percent pure Colombian cocaine and fill five duffle bags with a million dollars neatly stacked in each, even after weighing the dope twice.

It was a kilo short, but Junior thought nothing of the little loss. As much dope as he had, that was like losing a $5 bag. Besides, he was ready to go party with Spider and get some females.

Within five minutes, Junior and Spider were in his black, bulletproof BMW 745, followed by a black Suburban, on their way to Red Light, a new club that had quickly turned into the City of Visions hottest spot. Club Red Light was a black club, but it was Junior's favorite place to go when he went into town on business.

Spider was almost forty, with slick black hair and a spider web tattoo on his face—the last thing anyone saw before he killed them. Spider always kept a close eye on his thirty-three-year-old boss. He wasn't into the rap music the club played like Junior, but he figured it was the safest place for him. The Italians wouldn't try to kill Junior there and risk a war with the blacks and the Colombians at the same. Spider took a shot of tequila as he watched Junior get a lap dance from a thick, caramel-skinned female in their private section in the club. *It's going to be a long night,* Spider thought. He unscrewed the cross pendant that hung on a chain around his neck, where he stashed his cocaine and mini spoon. He quickly took a hit up his nose.

Junior got nothing but love in the club, and his private section was full of buckets of Cristal. Sexy black females walked in and out of his section like a revolving door, ready to do whatever Junior wanted, right there on the spot.

Junior's two armed bodyguards were guarding the door,

screening everyone who came in, but when the pretty light caramel-skinned female wearing a red fitted dress and six-inch heels approached, they just stepped to the side. Her presence quickly caught everybody's attention, including Junior's. He quickly moved the female off his lap and jumped to his feet.

The lady in red looked at Junior, who was dressed in an all-white Versace outfit, with matching white loafers. "I knew you'd be here drinking up all the Cristal and stealing all the bitches," she said as she approached him.

"Aisha, baby, you know this is what I do, ma," Junior said, taking the female into his arms and embracing her. "As a matter of fact, Juan, go buy the bar. Drinks on me tonight!" Junior demanded to one of his bodyguards, who wasted no time following his orders. Junior loved showing off for the manager of the club. Ms. Aisha was one of the finest black females he'd ever seen. Even though she was thick in all the right places, she was firm all over, and she had brown eyes he could just die in. He was really impressed by her hustling skills. *I wish I had a female like her,* he thought to himself, pushing her long black hair away to uncover her pretty face as they broke their embrace. Junior knew they would never work out though. He smiled at the devil in the red dress, who slapped one of the thong-clad females on her ass as she walked by, making the girl giggle. "You got more females than me, lady," Junior said.

"I sure do!" Aisha quickly snapped back, causing them

both to laugh.

Their laughter was quickly cut short by automatic gunfire and screams from outside the private room in the club. Junior's remaining bodyguard quickly jumped into action, pulling his .40-caliber out and taking a defensive position outside the door. Spider was pushing females out with one hand and waving his nickel-plated .45 automatic in the other, till nobody was remained in the room but Spider, Junior, and Aisha.

"Tony, what's happening!" Junior demanded of his six-six, 280-pound bodyguard. He pulled his black .45 from his pocket and made his way to the door behind Spider and Tony.

The crowd in the club split like the Red Sea, leaving only a hooded man standing there. He had thin dreads hanging down from under his hood, and he held a smoking AK-47 over his bloody victim, Juan, Junior's bodyguard. There was no time to fire back as the hooded figure quickly blended in with the fleeing crowd.

"Juan's dead!" Spider yelled to Junior.

Junior's mind was racing, but the cocking of a gun from him behind cleared his head, and a chill went down his spine. When he quickly turned around, there was Aisha, holding a nickel-plated 380 with a pearl handle clutched in her hand, like she was ready to kill.

"Out the back door! Let me handle this!" Aisha demanded.

Junior had thought she was going to kill him, but he

quickly pulled himself back together. "Let's go! Fuck him!" Junior demanded, putting his crew into instant motion.

Within seconds, they were out the door without a second guess or a goodbye. Their cars were waiting in the alley for quick escapes, and this one of those. They entered the alley rapidly but with caution, not knowing who could be waiting for them out there.

"Hurry! Follow us!" Junior demanded to the bodyguard, while he jumped into the driver seat of his BMW.

The black BMW pulled off down the alley, leaving the club behind, followed by an all-black Suburban with his bodyguard in it, along with enough ammo to take out a small army. Junior had the pedal to the floor, and his turbocharged BMW turned a ten-minute trip to the highway into a five-minute one.

Spider was geeked up off the cocaine, but his common sense kicked in. "Slow down, Junior!"

But Junior ignored him and continued driving like a madman, leaving his follower almost two blocks behind. He only stopped because he was sitting at the red light before the highway ramp. "We gon' kill whoever did this!" Junior said, mad as hell that someone had crossed him.

When the light turned green, Spider began speaking, but he couldn't even get his words out before he looked in the passenger mirror and saw that a police car had somehow gotten in between them and the bodyguards' car and was pulling them over. "Hurry! Give me your gun!" Spider said, knowing he was registered to carry a firearm.

They didn't waste time pulling over to the side of the road, as that was the least of Junior's concerns. The bodyguard didn't know what to do, so he just fell back a little bit and watched for anything strange. He got paid to kill, and that was what he was going to do. The officers didn't get out of the car right away; they just sat behind them like they were waiting on something. Five minutes later, the bodyguards found out what they were waiting on: Police cars came from every direction, surrounding them quickly.

Junior and Spider sat there calmly, knowing the police didn't have shit on them. At least ten officers had taken their positions in the street with their guns out, and Junior and Spider were ordered out the vehicle and down on their knees, then handcuffed right there in the street.

"What the fuck is this all about, Officer!" Junior snapped at the blond-haired officer who was searching him.

"We got a call about shots fired out of a black BMW!" the officer replied.

Junior didn't say anything else; he remembered the guns in the car under the passenger seat as he watched a couple of officers searching the vehicle.

"Gun!" one of the officers said when he found the weapons under Spider's seat.

"Those are mine, Officer. They're both registered to me!" Spider quickly said with confidence.

"How long is this going to take, Officer? I got shit to do!" Junior said, trying to stop laughing at the police, who were still searching the car.

The officers opened the trunk of the car and waved the blond-haired officer over.

Junior and Spider didn't know what the officers were looking at as they began whispering to each other. "What the fuck are they doing?" Junior whispered to Spider.

There was no response needed as they both watched the blond-haired officer reach in the trunk and pull out the tan, red scorpion-stamped kilo of cocaine that had been missing from the cocaine weigh-in at the warehouse earlier that night.

Both of the men's hearts dropped out of their chests and into the pits of their stomachs. They looked at each other, speechless, neither knowing how the missing brick of cocaine had gotten into the trunk.

The blond-haired officer approached, holding the kilo of cocaine in his hand. "You both have the right to remain silent!" the officer said, nearly laughing at them.

Spending the night in the musty feet-smelling county jail was not what Junior or Spider had planned, but they had no choice. They had to wait to go to bond court in the morning.

Man, am I ready to get out of here and go straight to my private plane and head back to Colombia, Junior thought to himself as he stood next to his lawyer, Eddie Gates.

Eddie was a clean-cut, dark-haired white man. He was dressed in a $5,000 suit and $2,000 matching shoes. The Shark, as he was known, only represented high-end criminals. His retainer fee alone, just to talk to him, was $20,000, but he was worth every dollar. "Your Honor, my client was visiting, drove a friend's car, and here we are. What say we just dismiss these crazy claims and save us all a lot of money and time and get this man back home?" the Shark said to the red-headed lady judge, using his charm on her.

Even though the judge found him attractive and had spent many nights with her fingers deep inside her pussy thinking about him, she kept her composure and turned her attention toward the fiery young Latina D.A., who had started speaking.

"Mr. Carlos is charged with possession of 1,008 grams of cocaine. He is the son of a known Colombian cartel leader. He was arrested speeding away from a murder scene, and officers recovered the drugs and two guns from the car he was driving. Those weapons are currently being run for ballistics, to see if they have anything to do with the shooting that Mr. Carlos was fleeing from," Ms. Ramos said in her Latina accent, turning and looking at the Shark and his client. Ms. Ramos was a hot, sexy, new D.A. She was five-four, with long, straight black hair that would've hung down to her ass had she not wrapped it up in a bun. Her perfect light brown complexion showed every bit of her black and Mexican heritage, and she had curves in all the right places. She had quickly made a name for herself with a twenty and zero conviction record in only ten months.

Junior wanted to fuck her bad. *And I just might after all this is over,* he thought to himself, looking back over at Ms. Ramos, making sure he made eye contact.

"Your client was caught red-handed, Counselor, and there are possible charges pending. I can't just let Mr. Carlos walk out of here. I'm sorry, Mr. Gates," the judge said, hoping deep down inside that it wouldn't mess up her chances to fuck him one day. "Bail recommendations for Mr. Carlos?" she asked the D.A. and the lawyer.

"I ask that my client be released on his own recognizance!" Mr. .Gates quickly shouted out. "My client has no priors, and—"

Ms. Ramos quickly cut him off. "I want to remind the court that Mr. Carlos has no address here!" Ms. Ramos said. "You let him go now, and he will flee the country before proper justice can be served!"

"Well, what is your suggestion, Counselor?" the judge asked Ms. Ramos.

"I ask that bail be set at one million dollars. If Mr. Carlos makes bail—which I know he will—I ask that he render his passport till our pending investigation is cleared up," Ms. Ramos answered.

"Is that all, Counselor?" the Judge asked

Ms. Ramos continued, "I also ask that since Mr. Carlos has no residence here, he should be put under house arrest at a hotel of his choice, all expenses paid for federal marshals to watch him, but his living expenses will be on him."

"Your Honor, that's ridiculous! The idea alone is stupid,

and for anybody to even consider something like that is as stupid as the one who thought of it!" Mr. Gates said, clearly upset.

"Bail shall be set at a million dollars, and Mr. Carlos will comply with all bail terms. Anyone who can pay a million dollar cash bail can surely foot a hotel bill!" the judge shot back at Mr. Gates, slamming her gavel down. Even though she wanted a piece of him, she didn't want him bad enough to let him disrespect her in her courtroom. *Maybe in my bedroom, but definitely not in here,* she thought to herself as her bailiff called the next case.

Junior wasn't happy with the decision, but that was only because he hated to lose at anything, A hour after the bond hearing, Junior had posted the million dollar-bail, and he was supposed to report to a hotel within the hour, but instead, he was on his way to the airport to leave the country, never to return. He knew he didn't need a passport to get into his country.

Junior's three-car caravan pulled into the airport hangar. The three black Suburbans turned in front of the private jet.

Junior wasted no time jumping out of the second truck, ready to get back home. Little did he know that his eagerness would get the better of him. He was moving so fast that he didn't even notice his pilot wasn't out to greet him as he approached the steps of the plane. Junior began climbing the stairs, but someone appeared at the door of the plane, stopping him dead in his tracks. Junior couldn't believe what he saw as he looked up. His mind was going 100 miles an hour, and his heart skipped a beat. Junior knew he had fallen into a trap; he had gotten caught slipping. *Out of all things, I let a female outsmart me,* he thought to himself, putting his hands up in surrender. The next sound he heard was the sound of police sirens, approaching fast.

"You still have fifteen minutes to report to your hotel, Mr. Carlos!" Ms. Ramos said, looking down at Junior from the top stairs of his private jet.

"Well, I'm heading there right now. I just came to get a few things off my jet before I check in," Junior replied, laughing.

"I figured that, so I wanted to ensure your safety and escort you there personally," Mr. Ramos said, walking down the stairs as she watched the four black Yukons with police lights, filled with U.S. marshals, pulling up to escort Junior and his caravan .

"I wouldn't have it any other way!" Junior said, retreating back to his truck. He was furious that he had gotten beat twice in one day by the same person. Junior thought matters couldn't get any worse, but when he tried to stay at his usual two hotels, they were suddenly booked for the rest of the month. Surprisingly, they both recommended the recently renovated penthouse at the Waltz Hotel. Junior hated that he had lost control of his situation. He stuck his rolled $100 bill back in the pile of cocaine and took another hit. Just as he finished, the room door came open.

"Junior, are you ready to party or what?" Spider said,

entering the room.

"Hell yeah!" Junior said, wiping the excess cocaine from his nose. Junior couldn't believe he'd almost had Spider killed when the state dropped the drug charges against him and left the weight on Junior. When stuff like that happens, somebody usually done told on you, but that wasn't the case with Spider, and he was just as surprised as Junior was when the charges were dropped. "Where's the bitches?" Junior asked, following Spider out of the room.

"They just arrived!" Spider replied, leading him toward the females and their pimp, all of whom were waiting in the massive living room of the penthouse.

As they approached, Junior could see he was going to have a ball that night. The two sexy white females had tan likes, like they'd just come from Florida. One was blonde, and the other was brunette. The brunette was wearing a black fitted mini-skirt and long black heels to match, and the blonde was dressed exactly the same, except her outfit was pink.

"What's happening, Junior?" the six-three, light-skinned man named Razor said, shaking hands with Junior.

"Good to see you, my friend!" Junior replied. Junior had met Razor through Aisha, and he liked the way Razor did business. Razor always kept a fresh face for Junior like he asked, and he always had some bad bitches. Junior looked at the two Barbie dolls he had for the night.

"This is Star," Razor said, pointing toward the blonde, "and this is Cherry," he finished, pointing at the brunette, who was sucking a cherry Blow Pop like it was a dick, enticing Junior.

"Hi, ladies," Junior said, pausing enjoying the lollipop show. "My name is Junior." He opened his arms, inviting the ladies to embrace him.

They wasted no time in finding their way into his arms. "Hey, Junior!" the ladies said simultaneously while they rubbed his chest.

Their greeting was ended abruptly by an approaching U.S. marshal. "Mr. Carlos, you have another guest named Aisha here to see you. What should I tell her?"

"What do you mean what should you tell her? Send her in, stupid!" Junior said, snapping at the officer.

The officer quickly retreated to get Aisha.

Junior could hear Aisha her still cussing out the security as she entered. "How you doing, beautiful?" Junior said, laughing as he greeted Aisha.

She was dressed in a gray business outfit, standing there with her hands on her hips, looking like a schoolteacher. Aisha's style was different every time Junior saw her. The long black hair she'd had last time they'd seen each other at the club was now shoulder length and honey blonde, but no matter how her style changed, her sexiness was undeniable.

"Aisha, don't come in here with that bullshit," Razor said, joking with her.

"Nigga, don't let my sophisticated look fool you. I will cut you," she quickly shot back, causing everybody to laugh. "I see I'm right on time for the party," Aisha said, looking the two females up and down.

"Yes, indeed you are. Me and the ladies are about to go enjoy the hot tub. Would you care to join us?" Junior responded.

"It has been a long day. I could use some relaxation," Aisha said, reaching in her black Louis Vuitton purse and pulled out her red Bic lighter and a tightly rolled Blackwood cigar, full of some weed with a smell so strong he almost thought the blunt had already been lit. "After you, Junior," Aisha said, lighting her blunt and taking her six-inch heels off before following Junior and the two ladies toward the room with the hot tub.

The hot tub room looked like something straight out of a movie. Two of the walls were made entirely of windows, offering a view out across the city. The hot tub was more like a mini-pool, and the steam from the water filled the room, creating a rainforest effect.

"I like this, Junior!" Aisha said, passing her blunt to him.

He quickly grabbed the cigar and began smoking as he responded, "I'm happy you like it. They say this room was just built a few months ago, and I'm the first one who gets to use it." Of course he was just bragging, since he didn't know when it had really been built.

Their conversation was interrupted by the blonde. "Where can I freshen up?" she asked.

"Right over there, sweetheart," Junior said, pointing

her toward the bathroom.

The blonde quickly made her way to the bathroom. She turned the sink water on and let the toilet seat down like she was going to use the bathroom, but instead she reached under the sink and retrieved a .40-caliber handgun from the holster hidden there, right where Razor said it would be. She looked in the huge full-body mirror on the wall, watching herself cock the gun. She couldn't help but laugh to herself, remembering how Razor had paid her and her friend Cherry a mere $10,000 a piece to kill Junior, as if they were some naïve white girls who didn't know any better. Little did Razor know, playing the role of naïve white girls was exactly what made them the top two hitters in The Reapers death squad. Star actually felt bad that she had to kill Razor, especially since he had been fucking her all week like she had never been fucked before. "Damn!" she said, thinking out loud. She instantly became wet thinking about him digging deep inside her. *But this is business, and business is never personal,* she thought to herself, aiming the gun at the mirror like she was taking aim at her reflection. All she had to do now was give her girl some time to work her magic, and then she would go in and clean everything up.

* * *

Junior stood by the room door, trying to adjust the switch on the wall that controlled the amount of steam in the rainforest room. Junior had partied in there many times before, and the steam had never filled the room like that. It was thick and made it impossible to see anything below his knees. If the water hadn't been bubbling in the hot tub, he wouldn't have been able to see it. Junior thought about getting it fixed, but the thought left his mind as the brunette, Cherry, started peeling off her black skirt, till she was down to her matching lace panties and bra, then got in the awaiting hot tub.

Cherry pointed toward Aisha and motioned with her finger, telling Aisha she wanted her to come and join her.

Aisha wasted no time making her way toward the hot tub, pulling off her suit jacket and blouse. She slowly unzipped her tight skirt and let it fall to the floor at her feet and stepped out of it.

Junior felt his nature rise instantly, looking at Aisha's lime-green thong disappear in between the most perfect ass he had ever seen.

Aisha looked back at Junior and giggled at him before she took a seat on the side of the hot tub, hanging her legs down in the water. Aisha quickly spread her thighs apart as Cherry found her way in between her thighs. She slowly rubbed up her thighs until she found exactly what she was looking for—a syringe taped to the front side of Aisha's thigh. Cherry quickly grabbed it and tucked it in the side of her panties that she still had on. Aisha wasted no time grabbing the back of Cherry's head with one hand and pulling her panties to the side with the other, giving the white girl a face full of her sweet black pussy. Cherry had never been with a female before, but Junior couldn't tell that from the way she licked and sucked all over Aisha's pussy, trying to get every drop of her sweetness.

"Eat that pussy, bitch!" Aisha said, grinding her pussy all over the girl's face, ready to explode in her mouth.

Cherry was so caught up in what she was doing that she didn't even realize Junior had gotten in the hot tub until she felt his dick pushing deep inside her from behind.

"OOOOh shit! I'm going to cum!" Aisha said as her body began trembling, causing her to grab Cherry's head and pull her face deeper in her pussy as she exploded her juices into Cherry's mouth.

Junior was so turned on that he just pounded inside Cherry, making her scream his name.

"Junior, Junior, Junior!" she yelled.

Junior pounded harder and harder until he couldn't take it no more and released his load inside the condom he was wearing. Junior quickly pulled his dick out of her, trying to recover, but Cherry quickly turned around and stuck him in his leg with the syringe and pushed its contents into him. Junior did his best to yell, but whatever she had put in his body had an instant effect. He clutched the left side of his chest like he was having a heart attack. Within seconds, he looked like he was doing the dead man's float on his back in the water. His eyes rolled back in his head, and his body went limp.

* * *

Spider and Razor stood at the full bar the in the penthouse, sipping a glass of $1,000-a-bottle tequila. Spider didn't trust Razor as far as he could see him, so when he visited, he kept him close as possible. "So where are the rest of the ladies?" Spider asked as the two men finished taking a shot.

"They should've been here. You know some hoes just don't follow directions," Razor shot back, causing the two men to laugh.

Even though Spider was laughing on the outside, he was only hiding his paranoia. With all the security and marshals up there, he knew it would be suicide for anybody to try and get to Junior, but considering the last week's events, Spider wasn't going to take any chances. He adjusted his .45 automatic with the custom spider web handgrip. He had it tucked in plain sight in the front of his pants, and he made sure Razor saw his gun every time he came over. It was clear he was sending an I-wish-you-would-try-something message.

Razor just smiled at Spider, amused by his gesture.

Spider wanted to wipe that smile off Razor's face, as he found himself squeezing his gun handle tighter. He was filled with anger, but he quickly caught himself and released his grip. He didn't know that would prove to be the biggest mistake of the last eight days.

Razor barely let Spider's fingertips get off the gun before he made his move. Razor's speed was like nothing Spider had ever seen before as he snatched the gun from the front of Spider's pants.

Spider did his best to reach for the gun, but by the time his hand reached for it, the .45 came crashing into the side of his face with so much force he thought his jaw was broken. Spider almost fell to his knees, but Razor quickly put him in a headlock with one arm and pressed the cold steel of the .45 against the side of his aching head. Spider was out on his feet, but the yelling from one of the officers brought him back around.

"Put the gun down and get on the floor!" the officer demanded.

Spider didn't know what was worse: having his own gun used against him or looking down the barrel of the seventeen machineguns that were pointing at him and Razor. Spider wanted to be tough, but he knew the situation could get out of hand real quick. Junior's goons, who were mixed in with the U.S. marshals, were aiming guns at them, and they'd been given direct orders to kill any threat at all cost.

"I'm not going to tell you to put the gun down again!" the officer yelled again.

"Come on, Razor! No harm, no foul. You put the gun down, and we'll act like this never happened," Spider murmured, talking through the pain that shot through his face with each word.

The response Spider got sent an instant chill down his spine: Razor just began laughing like it was all some kind of game to him.

This is not going to end pretty, he thought to himself, but to his surprise, the vice-like grip around his neck released, and Razor let him fall to his knees.

"Drop the gun and get on the floor!" the officer said as the man had released his hostage.

Razor put his hands up and let the gun just dangle from his finger as he got on his knees next to Spider.

"You know, I'm going to have fun killing you," Spider whispered to Razor.

Razor seemed to be looking at his watch as he lowered his arm to put the gun on the floor. "I advise you to duck!" Razor replied, sending confusion through the mind of Spider.

"Duck?" Spider said, thinking out loud.

The next thing he knew, the whole room went pitch black. Sounds of panic and gunfire filled the room, only it wasn't them doing the shooting. The mini-gun from the apartment across the street sent two to three rounds ripping through the glass wall of the penthouse suite, sparing no one or nothing in its path. The penthouse suite lit up like the Fourth of July, as security and the marshals began letting off gunfire, shooting into the darkness. The screams almost drowned out the gunfire as the relentless mini-gun continued to spray back and forth, chopping its victims in half with ease, until the once lively suite was now full of a chilling dead silence.

* * *

Star was a trained hitter, but she was caught off guard

by the lights going out and the sounds of machinegun fire coming from the other room. *Something has definitely gone wrong,* she thought to herself as she stood in the dark bathroom, but her thoughts were interrupted by the dim back-up lights coming on. She wasn't about to wait around and get killed, so she gripped her .40 caliber with one hand and slowly turned the doorknob, ready to finish her mission. The Jacuzzi room was very dim with the back-up light on, and the steam looked like fog in the midnight air. It reminded Star of a jungle at night, like something she'd seen on the Discovery Channel. She looked around as she slowly crept through the room; she didn't see anybody, including her friend Cherry.

The steam had completely covered the hot tub, but she remembered where it was, and she could still hear the bubbles gurgling in the water. She could see something where the water was, but she could barely make it out. Star bent down and pushed the tip of the gun against whatever it was in the water, but it didn't move. She then reached down with her other hand and grabbed it. Long, thick hair filled her hands as she pulled whoever it was in the water, only to have the head of her friend almost come off in her hands.

"Hey!" a whispered voice said from behind her, startling her.

Star's reflexes were fast as lightning. She swung around with the .40 caliber, ready to squeeze the trigger at whomever was behind her, but her move was cut short by a left hook to her eye that knocked the gun out of her hand and sent her to the floor. The punch caught her off guard, and she didn't even see where it had come from, but she quickly gathered her thoughts and was ready to strike back. To her surprise nobody was there. Star jumped to her feet, looking around the room with only one eye open since her right eye was quickly swelling closed by the second. Star's killer instinct was hungry as she looked around and listened for any sound, ready to attack and punish whoever had done the damage to her face. She didn't know if she was hurting more from her swollen eye or the fact that she had been outwitted by Razor and Aisha. Then, she heard the sound that would end her life.

Aisha seemed to jump right out of the floor in front of Star, hidden by the steam.

Star did her best to put up a defense, but she wasn't quick enough. Aisha swung a backhand with the straight razor she had in her hand and sliced right across Star's throat, like a hot knife going through butter. Blood sprayed in the air like a lawn sprinkler. Aisha merely laughed and delivered a roundhouse kick that hit Star in her chest, causing even more blood to squirt out of her neck, and knocked her into the hot tub with her dead friend Cherry. Aisha left her there, drowning on her own blood and water. Aisha would've loved to play some more, but she knew they had little time left to complete their mission. She made her way to where Junior's body was on the floor, hidden by the steam.

* * *

The streets below the hotel were in a frenzy. The people poured out of the hotel and onto the streets, afraid for their lives. Screams of fear and the annoying ringing of the fire alarm in the hotel filled the brisk night air. Sirens could be heard approaching fast, and within five minutes, the whole area was swarming with police cars, fire trucks, and ambulances. The lobby of the hotel was quickly evacuated, and in place of its rich guests was a police extraction team, headed by the two U.S. marshals that were posing as workers in the lobby.

Both of the marshals knew they were supposed to protect the target, but with all that gunfire, there was probably not any target left to protect. They took the lead position in front of the elevator, with ten tactical police officers behind them and ten more making their way up twenty flights of stairs to make sure nobody was coming down.

"It's now or never," the dark-skinned marshal said to his white partner, who looked just as scared as he did. The dark-skinned marshal reached for the elevator button to call for the elevator, but just as his finger got close enough to touch the button, the elevator from the penthouse began to move.

* * *

The FBI agents who'd been staking out Junior's place from the building across the street where the gunfire came from were still in shock that the gunfire had come from right above them. Two of the agents were so scared that they refused to leave the apartment; they wanted to wait for backup. The other agents didn't feel the same way, and they wasted no time leaving the apartment and heading toward the apartment upstairs where the gunfire came from.

They reached the hallway, approaching with caution. The older of the two, with salt-and-pepper hair, led the way, followed by the young blond agent. The whole building was silent except for a clicking sound coming from inside the apartment. The older one motioned for his partner to kick the door in. He complied with no hesitation, kicking the door off the hinges. They ran in, guns drawn, ready to kill anybody who got in their way, but what they saw stopped them dead in their tracks. The floor was covered with shell casings: The mini-gun had shot out well over 6,000 rounds. It was empty, but the six barrels kept spinning, as if it was still loaded. The agents now knew what the clicking sound was: The gun was set up remotely to just keep shooting at the penthouse across the street. They couldn't even walk without a spent shell casing crushing beneath their feet.

"You hear that?" the blond officer asked, making his way toward the kitchen "It sounds like a phone ringing."

The other officer couldn't hear anything at first, but as he followed his partner the sound grew louder and louder.

"It's coming from the refrigerator!" the blond agent

said. He opened the fridge where the ringing was coming from.

The two men instantly froze like they were playing freeze tag. They looked at the cell phone ringing on the top shelf, but it was the other thing in the refrigerator that washed the color out of their faces.

* * *

The elevator seemed to be going in slow motion, but finally, one of the two made its way to the lobby of the Waltz Hotel, where a crowd of officers were waiting. No matter how much training an officer received, nothing could have prepared them for the unexpected, and what was behind the elevator doors was definitely unexpected. The doors began to open slowly. The officers took aim, but they didn't know what they were aiming at, because thick black smoke poured out of the open elevator doors. A coughing sound emerged from the smoke, followed by a light-skinned marshal carrying a blood-covered black female with a gray dress suit on. The marshal's bloody face made him hard to identify. The officers relaxed.

"Hurry! Get them to an ambulance!" one of the head officers said. "Is there anybody else up there alive?" he asked the blood-covered marshal who walked through the parting sea of officers on his way to the ambulance.

"I think they're all dead," the marshal responded, sending chills down the officers' spines as they got ready to head to the penthouse.

"Those are our only two witnesses. Keep an eye on them!" the head officer yelled out.

The words barely got out of his mouth before the blast came from an explosion in the vacant apartment across the street, where the feds were doing surveillance. It felt like it was going to shake the hotel off its foundation. The windows of the Waltz exploded from the force of the blast, sending officers flying everywhere. People ran through the streets in panic, while thick black smoke came from three floors of the apartment building across the street. Nobody in the city had seen devastation and bloodshed of that caliber before. Unfortunately for them, it was just a beginning. There was more to come, and it was definitely going to get worse before it got better.

CHAPTER THREE

Deadly Secrets

WWW.GSTREETCHRONICLES.COM

Three days had passed, and the stench of death and gun smoke seemed to still linger through the air outside the Waltz Hotel. The black Crown Vic pulled in front of the Waltz, and the young black rookie detective with the tight fade quickly put the car in park, almost making his pale white, bald-headed partner spill his coffee on the *City Times* newspaper in his lap.

The white veteran detective, Dooley, couldn't do nothing but shake his head. He wasn't fond of his new partner's driving, but he was even less fond of the newspaper headlines: "31 Dead, 2 Missing, Police Still Baffled."

"Fuck this! Whoever's responsible for this is sitting somewhere laughing at us," said the black detective, Hill, interrupting Dooley's train of thought.

"You're right about that shit!" Dooley quickly responded. He had an idea who was responsible for it. Dooley usually didn't deal with cases like those, as his job was to hunt down serial killers, but with the magnitude of death in this situation and the fact that a weapon used at the massacre at the Waltz was the same one used by the one serial killer who'd evaded him for the last five years, he was now the lead detective on the case.

The two detectives got out of the car and headed inside to investigate the crime scene for the seventh time in three days. Dooley had OCD when it came to crime scenes, and this case was no different. The two officers approached the double elevators. An officer was waiting outside, and there was yellow crime scene tape behind him. Even though Dooley didn't like what had been said about the case in the news, it was true. The officers had been made a fool of the night of the shooting, and they had let the killers walk right out the front door, posing as a U.S. marshal and a wounded female victim. Nobody remembered their faces due to the fact that they were covered with blood, and they had used smoke grenades in the elevator and the stairwell to slow law enforcement down for hours, making them think there was a fire in the building. They'd used a perfectly timed explosion across the street as a diversion, so they could disappear into the night under the camouflage of chaos. The only thing Dooley didn't know was where the hell Junior and Spider were. He was so immersed in his thoughts that he almost didn't hear the officer guarding the elevator when he greeted them.

"Morning, Detectives," the skinny white officer said.

"Morning," Dooley and Hill detectives replied at the same time.

The officer quickly hit the button to summon the elevator and removed the yellow tape so the detectives could get in the elevator when it arrived. The hotel was still closed still, so it seemed odd to Dooley that the elevator had to come from the penthouse floor, but before he could say anything, the officer spoke again.

"It sure has been busy here this morning."

Dooley wasted no time responding. "Busy? What do you mean?"

"Well, three crime scene guys went up about ten minutes ago. Said they are supposed to clean the place up or something."

The detectives both looked at each other, knowing there wasn't supposed to be a crew in there for a couple days. The detectives drew their guns without hesitation.

The started officer hoped he hadn't messed up. "But... well, they had paperwork and white biohazard suits on!" he said, knowing he was lying about the paperwork part.

"That doesn't matter!" Dooley said as he tried read the young officer's name on his badge. "Krypowski, I need you to calm down and don't let nobody out this elevator," Dooley demanded, and then he and Hill jumped in the waiting elevator to ride to the penthouse. In his eagerness, Dooley had forgotten one thing he should've told the officer: call for backup. He tried using his phone, but the elevator was blocking the signal, and it was too late to correct the problem.

The detectives took positions inside the elevator door, with their backs against the wall and their guns in their hands. Dooley looked across at the eyes of his six-two rookie partner; Hill towered over Dooley by about four inches, and he looked ready, holding on to his Glock 9. Dooley hoped the rookie's looks weren't just deceiving. He cocked the hammer back on his .38 snub-nose revolver as the elevator came to a stop, reaching its destination. The doors opened, and the detectives made their way out slowly, being precautious, especially since the door to the penthouse was wide open. Everything sounded quiet as the two detectives made their way in the door of the penthouse, but a sound from behind them made them both turn around quickly, ready to shoot. The detectives held their fire, realizing it was just the elevator door closing behind them. The detectives both took a deep breath. Their hearts were really pounding, but they continued bravely inside the penthouse.

They could see that nothing had been cleaned. Blood and glass were everywhere. They had been through every inch of the penthouse over and over again over the last few days, and that was clear from the way they swiftly cleared room by room. It wasn't until they got to the bathroom in the hot tub room that everything seemed to change instantly. The two detectives stood there, frozen at what they saw. The big wall mirror in the bathroom was really a door to a little room just big enough for a few people to fit in, and all the walls were covered with soundproofing.

"Let's go!" Dooley said to his partner as he turned around and ran toward the elevator. He was sure his suspects must have been going down in the other elevator while they were coming up in the other one. When they reached the elevators, to their surprise, the elevator they had just gotten out of was on its way back up, and the other one seemed to be in the lobby. Dooley couldn't believe that the whole time, their missing two victims, Junior and Spider, had been hid right under their noses. He just hoped Krypowski had been capable of holding them off in the lobby until they got there. His hope was quickly deflated when the elevator door opened.

There was Krypowski, lying face down on the floor, with his hands cuffed behind his back and his gun missing. "I'm going to get in trouble for this, huh?" the handcuffed officer said in shame, knowing he had fucked up.

The detectives just shook their heads at each other in disgust, neither of them having any doubt in their minds that they were being laughed at now for sure.

* * *

The laughter filled the back of the white van as it pulled out of the empty Waltz Hotel parking lot. The driver took his contamination mask off that had hidden his identity. His grin displayed his gold teeth in the mirror as his son No'fere and niece Tish (aka Razor and Aisha) rejoiced over pulling off the kidnapping of Junior and Spider. *Stage one is completed, but we've still got a ways to go,* Red thought to himself, proud of his son and his niece, just like the first time they'd pulled a hit together. It was a gratifying moment for him, similar to the pride a parent would feel watching their kid walk across the platform for their graduation. He couldn't do anything but smile as it replayed in his mind, as if it had happened yesterday.

It had been seven years. With King in jail and him and Red bowing out of the dope game, there were dealers popping up all over the streets, and Red had learned a method of extorting all of them. Red's reputation in the streets made many just pay the toll to play. They'd rather pay Red than have the maniac on their heels. The first time Red went to see anyone, it was all business. If he went back again, they didn't have to worry about their being a third visit. The bottom line was, pay or die.

The only one who hadn't gotten the memo was a fake mob boss named Billy "The Banker." The Banker was a young, hot-headed Italian who lived by his own rules. He got his name from knocking over banks when he was in his teens. After doing a ten-year stretch at eighteen, he came home with nothing more than a cocaine plug he had come across in prison. The Italian mafia had just begun their movement with the cocaine and had locked most of the city up. Their only problem was the Banker. The mob offered a hand to him, hoping he'd join the family, considering he was Italian, but the Banker refused. The Banker had a Colombian plug that had him doing serious bank numbers, and he was their number one earner. He knew the Italians weren't going to let him continue to operate with them, so he said, "Fuck them." The Italians were insulted and tried to shut him down, but they underestimated his power and his general disregard for human life. He ordered the hit on five mafia members' families. At each of those crime scenes, a bank deposit slip was left, letting them and anybody else know he was responsible. The mafia backed off after that and just let him make his money.

It had been a week since Red had come down to the Banker's pizza shop he used as a front to cover up his dirty money. The Banker spent his days there conducting business, surrounded by six of his goons. Red had given the Banker a week to think about the offer. Red told the Banker he wanted 40 percent of his weekly drug money. The Banker couldn't believe the nerve of a single black guy, coming in and telling him to give up 40 percent of his profits, and he'd been laughing on the inside all week thinking about it, but the laughter was about to stop when Red came walking through the door a week later, just like he said he would.

It was almost closing time when Red came through the doors of the pizza parlor. The young, pretty black girl who had been working there for two weeks, along with the Banker's daughter, were cleaning up by the register area. Red only looked at them for a second as he entered with his long black cornrows draping down his back. He was dressed all in black, including black leather gloves.

The Banker's security quickly met him. Red gave no resistance as he was searched for weapons before he went any further. The six-five, 300-pound bodyguard was the Banker's biggest security man, but standing next to Red, he didn't look as intimidating.

The Banker waved for his security to let the man pass. He was sitting in his booth, dressed in an expensive black suit. There wasn't a strand of dark hair out of place, and his clean cut made him look like an actual banker straight off of Wall Street. His two under bosses sat at his side, and standing around them closely with their guns in hand were his other three goons, ready to shoot the moment they saw Red.

"This how you greet a business partner?" Red said, laughing as if the whole thing was a joke.

"Business partner, huh?" the Banker replied, laughing as well. He found humor in Red's comment. "Put those guns up!" the Banker demanded. He noticed a light-skinned young man come in with a pizza box in his hand, apparently bringing an order back.

Red began speaking again. "I sure hate that I had to come back down here in person, but I gave you a week, and I haven't heard from you. Either you just wanted me to come down here and pick my money up myself, or you saying fuck what I'm talking about. Either way, I'm not happy."

The Banker almost didn't know what to say. He was shocked by Red's aggressive comment, especially since Red was so sorely outnumbered and unarmed. "Fuck if you're unhappy and fuck your deal!" the Banker said, enraged with anger and feeling disrespected in front of his men. "So unless you tired of breathing, I suggest you turn around and walk out the door and never come back. If you do, you'll be leaving here in a box."

The Banker's security and his under bosses instantly tensed up, waiting on Red to make a move so they could kill him.

To their surprise, Red just smiled, displaying his gold teeth like he was pleased with the Banker's decision and amused by his threats. "Nice doing business with you," Red said as he turned and walked away.

The Banker's big goon that had searched Red stood in Red's path.

When Red walked right up to him and stood nose to nose, they looked like two heavyweight fighters. The look on Red's face said, *"I'll knock your bitch ass out."*

"Let him pass!" the Banker said, quickly diffusing the situation, just wanting Red to leave.

The goon starred for a couple more seconds, putting up a front like he was ready for some action but knowing damn well he was happy his boss had intervened and likely saved his ass.

"Pussy!" Red whispered to the fake goon as he walked by, like he could read the man's tiny little mind.

The Banker and his under bosses were laughing as Red walked away, feeling like they had won that little battle. The whole little situation had taken their attention away from the light-skinned boy who'd brought the pizza back. He and the black girl at the counter were arguing over his pizza being messed up while the Banker's daughter counted the order slips for the night so she could do the books.

"Every time I order from here, my food fucked up!" the boy said, sitting the pizza box on the counter.

"Well, sir, I'm sorry you feel that way. You keep telling me we messed up your order, but you still haven't told me how," the black girl replied with attitude.

The situation caught the Banker's attention, and he waved to his big goon to take care of it.

Red was just approaching the light-skinned customer with the Banker's goon about four steps behind when the light-skinned boy looked over at Red and began smiling just like him before he turned back to the black girl and started talking again. "Why tell you what's wrong with my pizza when I can show you?" he said, lifting the pizza box lid.

The goon was watching as the man opened the pizza box, ready to see what all the fuss was about, but as the lid came open, he could now see what the problem was: There was no pizza in the box—only two Glock .45s and a .357 revolver. The goon was so caught off guard by what he saw that he failed to pay attention to Red, who had stopped walking. Red never gave the goon a chance to get his thoughts together; he turned around with a whirlwind left hand that smashed into the lower right side of the goon's chin. The goon just fell over, asleep like a newborn baby before his back hit the floor.

The Banker and his goons were also caught off guard by what was going on, causing them to hesitate. That would cost them. Red's son No'fere, posing as the customer, and his niece Tish, posing as the register worker, snatched the two .45s out of the box with lightning speed. The Banker's daughter saw what was happening and reached for the shotgun that was hidden under the counter, but Tish shot her right in the middle of the back of her head, killing her instantly. No'fere stepped in front of his dad and squeezed off five shots. One of the goons was just pulling his gun out of his holster when three of their bullets ripped into his chest, slamming him into the wall behind him. The other goon that was standing next to him and caught a bullet high in the chest; another bullet went through his throat and out the back of his neck, severing his spine. The Banker's other Goon got off a couple shots in Red's and No'fere's direction, but he was shooting scared and missed by a long shot. The next breath he took out of his scared body was his last, as Tish squeezed off another round from her gun that landed right in the side of the man's head, leaving his brains hanging out as he died on his way to the floor. Just as she squeezed the trigger, the door from the kitchen flew open. The cook emerged from the back, wielding a shotgun, but he never got to use it, as Tish swung back his way, not missing a beat, and put two bullets in the side of the man's neck, sending blood squirting everywhere and the cook to an early grave.

Red quickly joined in the action, as if he was in competition with his son and niece. He grabbed his .357 out of the box and turned around, as if he wasn't even aiming, and pulled the trigger of the massive .357 two times. The Banker's under bosses never got the chance to return fire or get out of the booth before the .357 bullet landed smack dab in the middle of both of the men's foreheads, almost simultaneously leaving both of them in a dead slump.

The Banker tried to hide under the table. "Wait, wait!" he screamed, waving a white napkin with one hand, trying to surrender and hoping his hand didn't get shot off. The Banker slowly peeked his head out, only to see Red with Tish on his right side and No'fere on his left. "Please! I'll take your deal!" the Banker said, pleading for his life.

"I thought about what you said about the deal," Red said, then pausing before continuing, "and I've decided you right. Fuck a deal!" Red said.

"No, no, no!" the Banker pleaded as Tish and No'fere raised their guns, aiming at him.

They paid his cries no attention as they pulled there triggers until the Banker's body was full of holes.

Red just laughed. He was going to kill the man whether he had agreed to the deal or not because that hit was personal. Red just looked at his son and niece, proud of them.

Now, years later, he felt that same pride as he looked at them in the mirror. Red was so caught up in his thoughts that he almost didn't hear No'fere talking to him from the back of the van.

"Pops, why you smiling and shit? Don't start that weird shit," No'fere said, causing him and Tish to laugh.

"Don't start that get-you-fucked-up shit, No'fere," Red quickly replied, causing all of them to laugh. Even though they were laughing, Red just shook his head knowing two people in this world that weren't going to be laughing today and that was Junior and Spider, he thought to himself as continued to laugh on his way to their safe house.

* * *

It had been a long couple months for No'fere and Tish. They knew setting Junior up would be hard, but they also knew the only way to get him was to force him outside his normal pattern and make him play by their rules. Junior never would've guessed that everything—from the kilo in his trunk to the hotel he'd checked into—was part of a perfect setup. Tish and No'fere had pulled a lot of missions, but none with stakes so high. Junior had a lot of starving workers around, so it wasn't difficult for No'fere to talk one of the dock hands into selling him the kilo the police had found in the trunk, considering he'd paid double for it. Getting it in the trunk had been just as easy. While Junior and Spider were partying in the club VIP section, No'fere was breaking into their car to place the kilo in the trunk. Once it was in place, No'fere came back in the side door, slipped on a dreadlock wig, grabbed an AK-47, and waited in the shadows for Tish to get in position in the room with Junior and Spider.

The only thing that hadn't gone as planned was Junior sending his bodyguard to buy the bar out. The original plan was for No'fere to run up toward the room and shoot the bodyguard so none of the people at the club would get caught in a crossfire, but No'fere improvised. Before he made his move, he began shooting in the air, forcing people to scatter. It actually worked in his favor, as Junior's bodyguard didn't know what to do and never even got a chance to pull his gun out before No'fere had ran through the fleeing people and chopped the man down with the AK-47. Junior panicked, just as Tish and No'fere thought he would, and they used that moment for Tish to come off as the hero. When Junior turned around and saw her holding a gun, he thought his life was over, but when he saw she was on his side, they knew he would trust her. What they didn't know was that seconds after Junior and Spider fled from the club, Tish called the police and reported some men in a car with guns and gave them the license plate number.

Everybody knew Junior would try and leave the country once he got released from jail, and when he couldn't leave on his plane, his only option was to go to the Waltz Hotel, right where they wanted him. There weren't too many hotels someone as self-important as Junior would stay in, so getting him to the Waltz was as simple as booking all the rest of the penthouse suite in the city. One of Tish's high-end weed clients owned the Waltz, so when she offered to trade him pounds of cush for rent at his newly remodeled penthouse, he jumped at the deal, no questions asked. So, for two weeks before Junior checked in, Red and No'fere built a secret room behind the mirror in the bathroom, the perfect place to hide Junior and Spider while they walked right out the front door. Thanks to the Professor and the drug he'd created—the drug King had gone to jail to protect—they were able to keep Junior and Spider asleep for three days. The ketamine, also known as Special K, put them into an instant coma and slowed their heartbeats down that they could medically be considered dead.

Even though Tish and No'fere were skeptical about the Professor's drug working at first, it had done exactly what he'd claimed it would do. The only thing they had left to do now was bring Junior and Spider back from their drug-induced comas by injecting their hearts with a dose of adrenalin. The two of them entered the subzero meat locker where Junior and Spider were being held, stripped down and handcuffed by their ankles and wrists to metal chairs bolted to the floor.

"Now, uh, you heard what the Professor said, right? We got to make sure we stab him hard enough to break through his chest plate," No'fere said, stuttering his words out and revealing his nerves as he walked toward Spider. He was dressed in his Pelle Pelle down coat, all black, with black gloves and a black skullcap to match, and he carried an adrenalin-filled syringe. No'fere might have had all the precision of a surgeon with a gun in his hand, but stabbing a man in his heart with a needle wasn't his thing.

Tish just laughed at him, causing him to start talking some more.

"Why you all dressed up like you going to a club?"

No'fere asked, causing the both of them to stop right in front of their two victims. Junior was on the left side of the room, right in front of Tish, and Spider was to the right, with No'fere in front of him.

"Why you always hating, Fere?" Tish replied, calling him by the nickname she'd always called him since they were younger. Even though they were cousins, they had a bond like a brother and sister. Tish couldn't do nothing but shake her head, because he was right. After all, she was wearing her pink Pelle Pelle leather coat that hugged right above her hips, pink gloves, pink and white earmuffs ,tight white jeans, pink Gucci boots with white fur, and—to top it all off—a long, straight, pink wig with white highlights.

"Just make sure you do like the Professor said. We don't got no time to be fucking up, rock star," No'fere said with a little giggle.

As soon as his words left his mouth, Tish slammed the big needle into Junior's bare chest, puncturing his heart and filling it with the dose of adrenalin.

No'fere quickly followed suit, sticking Spider with the needle he had in his hand, refusing to be outdone by his cousin; they'd always had a healthy, relentless competitive nature, and things weren't about to change now.

Junior's seemingly lifeless body was quickly revived. His eyes popped open, and he took a deep breath of air and let out a scream of pain, since Tish had left the needle stuck in a few seconds longer than necessary.

Spider woke up the same way, except he didn't make a

sound. His resilience for pain had been well documented over the years, so his actions came as no surprise to No'fere or Tish.

"What the fuck is going on, Aisha?" Junior asked, calling Tish by the only name he knew her as. Junior couldn't remember anything but getting into the hot tub with Tish and the white girl in the penthouse. Everything after that was a blank.

"I know what's not going on," Tish replied, looking down at his pathetic, shriveled-up dick. "Must be the cold air, right?" Tish teased before she let out her devilish laugh and took a seat on Junior's lap. Junior wanted to kill Tish, but he knew she had him down bad. Besides, he needed the body heat, since the subzero temperature was so cold to his skin that it felt like it was on fire.

"If it's money you want, I can give you ten times the amount the Italians can for turning me over to them," Junior said, pleading for his freedom and knowing in the back of his mind that if she ever let him free, he would surely kill her and the man he knew as Razor, who was standing behind Spider, not saying a word.

"Shhhhhhhhh!'" Tish said, putting her finger over Junior's lips to stop him from talking. "So how much is your life worth, Spider?" Tish asked, turning her attention to Spider, who looked calm, even under his dire circumstances.

"Fuck you, bitch!" Spider said, staring in the weak eyes of Junior, disgusted by the way he was pleading for his life.

Tish just laughed at Spider.

Her laugher made him angrier, causing him to try and break his handcuffs, which were so tight that blood was dripping from his wrists. "You think you muthafuckas scare me?" Spider said, pausing as he laughed at little under his breath before he continued. "You think some cold air is pain, bitch? I walk with the devil, and when I get out these handcuffs, I'll introduce you to him."

"See? I told you he's too tough for this," Tish said to No'fere, who didn't say anything as he bent down and picked something up off the floor.

Junior wondered what the silent No'fere had picked up, but the thought barely got a chance to cross his mind before his question was answered.

Spider saw Junior's once weak eyes look up and to his left, as big as silver dollars, causing Spider to quickly look to his left. He saw No'fere swinging a sledgehammer downward, like a construction worker. Spider's instincts made him attempt to move, but it was useless, as the steel end of the sledgehammer came crashing into his knee with so much force it shattered every bone in its path. The once resilient Spider let out a scream that he didn't even know existed in him. Then, he tried his best to regain his composure, but before he could No'fere brought the massive sledgehammer down on the same knee again, causing a bone to rip through Spider's skin.

Junior had never seen anything like it before, and he could swear he could feel pain in his own knee as he looked at Spider's, which looked like it was barely being held together by flesh.

No'fere quickly cocked the sledgehammer back again and took another swing, slamming it into the middle of Spider's chest again and again and again until it felt like it was stuck in his caved-in chest. Blood poured out of Spider's mouth as he gasped for air, but even that would do him no good at that point.

Junior couldn't believe how the once calm, quiet man who'd been letting the female do all the talking had instantly turned into a sledgehammer-wielding maniac, but what the man he knew as Razor did next was even more surprising.

No'fere looked like he was tired, and he was breathing hard as he let the heavy head of the sledgehammer rest on the floor. "I got fifty grand say I can knock his head clear off his shoulders," No'fere said, rubbing his hands together like he was just getting warmed up, while his victim's body barely had a few seconds of life in it.

"I'll take that bet!" Tish said, jumping off Junior's lap, excited.

No sooner than Tish got up, No'fere grabbed the sledge hammer once again and spun around in a circle, giving his swing extra momentum, doing his best to win the bet he'd just made. The sound of the sledgehammer connecting with the middle of the Spider's forehead sent a chill down Junior's spine upon impact. The force of the blow cracked Spider's head open like a cantaloupe and broke his neck, leaving his head hanging back far further than it should have, as if he had nodded off, only backward.

Junior had seen a lot of sick stuff in his lifetime, but nothing like that. He was almost too scared to breathe, so shocked he almost didn't feel the piss running down his leg.

"Now, I hope you're not as tough as your buddy, 'cause I sure hate to have to give this nigga a double-or-nothing bet," Tish said to Junior while she look at No'fere, who was shaking his head, disappointed he'd lost.

Junior just shook his head, too scared to say a word.

No'fere threw his sledgehammer over his shoulder as he and Tish began walking toward the door, knowing their work was done.

"Yeah, nigga. Let's go get my money," Tish said to No'fere ,who still couldn't believe he had lost.

"I'm gon' give you your money. Damn, you always sweating people," No'fere replied, causing the cousins to laugh as they closed the freezer door behind them.

The conversation would've continued between the two of them but they were interrupted by the approaching footsteps of a little black man with white hair, dressed in a lab coat. The man everyone knew as the Professor. "Did it work like I said it would?" he asked No'fere and Tish. "No need to answer," he said, showing his confidence.

Tish just laughed at the old man, knowing the Professor lived to talk shit.

"Don't make me drop these guns on you. I heard you

BEASTMODE 2

done lost a step over the years," No'fere said, putting his dukes up and messing with the Professor like he loved to do.

"Boy, the only step I'm going to lose is the one in your ass," the Professor replied before pulling his flask out of his pocket and taking at swig. "Come on. I got something for y'all." He turned and walked off through one of the three old meat packaging warehouses they ran their operations from.

Tish and No'fere quickly followed, knowing that if the Professor had something for them, it had to be good.

Within minutes, the three of them were outside the door of one of the other two warehouses. It didn't look like much from the outside or even when they first walked in, as the front only housed two old black Chevy Caprices that Red said used to belong to King. The Professor walked right past the cars to a door that led to the back part of the warehouse. Having a brilliant doctor/scientist from the 'hood definitely had its benefits, and one of them was what was behind that door.

The bright lights from inside the room were almost blinding, especially after walking through the rest of the dim warehouse, but the only sense they needed was their sense of smell, as the strong aroma of high-grade marijuana took the place of the old and musty-smelling warehouse. The room was full of plants that looked like trees, every strand of high-grade marijuana they could think of: hydro, Northern Lights, cush—you name it, he grew it.

The bright lights made the place feel like a summer day on Miami Beach, complete with a perfect breeze coming from the huge fans, blowing air through the Professor's secret garden. At any given time, he was growing 5,000 to 10,000 plants, so many it was difficult to walk through to his work area in the back, where he lived most of the time. It was somewhat like a lab, with two rooms. He used the dark room to make the marijuana go into harvest, and the other room he used to dry the marijuana by hanging it upside down from the ceiling, the final stage before being able to roll it up and smoke it. He only had a little furniture, including a long metal work table covered with loose marijuana and a big scale to weigh the marijuana be before he bagged it. There was also an old couch he slept on, and he had a TV with a built-in DVD player so he could watch his favorite movie, The Mack, over and over again.

Lined up nicely and neatly along the wall were twenty twenty-gallon garbage cans, each containing 100 vacuum-sealed pounds of only the finest of the marijuana he harvested, ready to be sold by Tish and No'fere for $5,000 to $6,000 a pound. The weed that didn't make the cut was thrown in a dumpster, which was almost full. Tish and No'fere always found a use for the discarded marijuana, proving that one man's trash was definitely their treasure.

The Professor was running a huge grow operation all by himself, turning millions of dollars in profit, and most would have charged an arm and a leg for such a service, but he didn't want anything in return except a place to work and do his research. The Professor was willing to do whatever he had to do to see that the little blue pill he had created, something King called the beast, would give him a chance to reap revenge on a government that had used him to kill his own people. That thought alone made the Professor take his flask out and take another sip. Only two people knew his dark secret: himself and King. The Professor briefly pushed the thoughts away so he could show Tish and No'fere what he had for them. "Now this is what I got for y'all!" he said, reaching for some freezer bags full of two different kinds of specially grown marijuana—a mix the Professor called purple kryptonite.

No'fere quickly stepped up and grabbed his bag and opened it, anxious to finally see the marijuana the Professor had been bragging about for a year now.

The Professor just watched No'fere and Tish as the young man and woman fondled through the green and purple buds of purple kryptonite, excited about their gift. He cracked a smile; seeing them happy made him happy, and he did his best to keep them smiling. It was the least he could do considering they were willing to die for a cause they knew very little about. The Professor quickly shook his flask, hoping there was a shot left in it. He could hear the liquor swishing around the inside the flask, his temporary relief. He put the flask to his lips, doing his best to wash the thought of his shameful secret out of his mind again, but the liquor had little effect on the memories that had already started to haunt him.

* * *

The Professor hadn't always been a doctor. His first love was science. He was a born genius, and by the time he turned eighteen, he had the intelligence of a rocket scientist. In that day and age, racism was heavy, but as smart as he was, the government wasn't about to let the color of his skin stop them from using his genius mind, so they did. The government put the eighteen-year-old Professor to work with a group of three white scientists who specialized in chemical warfare. The whites weren't fond of him at first, but one great mind recognizes another, and they soon found out The Professor was smarter than all three of them put together. The four scientist worked day and night, using their minds to create some things that still made the Professor sick to his stomach still to that day.

One of their first projects was a virus called A1. It was capable of shutting down a person's immune system, leaving the person's body defenseless against disease, which would eventually lead to an early death. It could be administered to a carrier, who would then unknowingly infect others, unaware it could be spread through blood or sexual fluids, thus creating a new carrier, and the process would continue till it was a widespread pandemic. They even joked around, calling it a silent killer, because by the time someone found out they were infected, it was already too late to do anything about it, and they'd likely infected others.

When the government told them to take a highly addictive drug, cocaine, which was popular in Colombia and was being used in medicine, and see how its addictive nature could be intensified, the young Professor was put to the challenge by his fellow scientist. He quickly accepted the challenge of that project, wanting to be accepted fully by his colleagues, and he took it farther than they would've of thought capable. The Professor researched and experimented until he came up with a method of cooking the cocaine in its powder form, which people were starting to sniff up their nose to get high at that time. When he cooked it with water and a powdery substance that would later be called baking soda, it turned the soft cocaine into a hard, rock-like substance that could be smoked, which increased the addictive nature and the high by ten times.

Even though the young Professor had proven himself to his colleagues far beyond their expectations and they acted like they finally accepted him, something still didn't seem right. It was as if everyone knew about an inside joke he wasn't in on. After a while, he decided to just blow it off. He blamed his paranoia on the one thing he never could get used: using humans like lab rats. Normally, they would've used animals, but the government insisted on seeing the actual results on humans, so they supplied them with those human lab rats, mostly homeless people, assuming they wouldn't be missed. They offered the vagrants free room and board and hot meals in exchange for trying out a new medicine that they claimed would help the United States. They didn't tell them that one of the side effects was death.

When the Professor had first started, he didn't care who or what they were using. He was just happy for the opportunity, a rare treat for a young black man. But after two years, he'd almost reached his breaking point. He didn't know relief was right around the corner. One day when he showed up at work, everything was shut down. The other scientists told him that government funding had been pulled, because they'd failed at all their projects. The young Professor wasn't mad about losing his job, but he was insulted to be called a failure, especially since he had plans to unveil a drug called K-9, a more powerful drug than any that had ever been produced. He had planned to bring it out to the government, but he was a perfectionist and wanted it to be perfect. The young Professor took his failure went back to school and became a doctor. He decided that after helping to create death, he should work to save lives. For the next thirty-plus years, he worked at a health clinic in a poverty-stricken community, helping and healing the less fortunate. He thought the more people he helped, eventually the ones he'd helped to hurt in the past might stop haunting his dreams. He constantly wondered if the government had found his deadly creations and put them to use. If they had, he knew he might have been responsible for millions of deaths. He never would've guessed such a nightmare was about to become his reality.

In early 1981, the Professor started noticing the beginnings of an epidemic in the United States, something called "acquired immune deficiency syndrome," otherwise known as AIDS. The Professor could have sworn the AIDS virus was the same one he'd help to create, the A1 virus. The only difference was that AIDS was far more aggressive than his. The Professor tried to brush it off as a coincidence, but he finally got his confirmation in 1984, when he turned on the television news.

"A new terrorist has shown its face in the United States. It has taken our streets hostage, and its name is crack. Cocaine is no longer the rich man's high. Now, the soft, powdery substance is being cooked into a hard rock form, which is smoked for an increased and more intense high. The worst-hit areas are poverty-stricken communities, in which 90 percent of the people are African-Americans."

The Professor couldn't believe what was happening. The government had used *him* to create a weapon of mass destruction, and its target was his very own people. He had seen symptoms of the drug use in some people he'd been treating lately, but he'd been living in denial, hoping it wasn't true. The burden of being responsible for the attack on his people drove him to drink heavily, doing his best to drown away the problem, but there was no use. He knew crack was a disease with no cure, and all he could do was watch helplessly as it destroyed the communities one by one. Not even the Professor could believe the primal effects that crack had in the 'hoods nationwide. Crack offered a young black man the opportunity to become rich overnight, and for many young blacks, that was the opportunity they'd dreamt about forever. Even if someone was uneducated or unable to shoot a jump shot, all they needed to know when it came to crack was how to count money, because the drug pretty much sold itself. Blacks quickly grasped the idea of getting rich quick and easy and began selling crack for a living, even to their own people. Babies were being born to mothers who'd been using the drug, passing their addiction to their children. Crack users were willing to do whatever it took to get the drug, even if they had to sell everything they had, including their kids and themselves. Crack dealers sold the drug relentlessly, the money and the power blinding them to the families they were destroying to get rich. Killing became an everyday thing, as gangs ran the drug trade like a Fortune 500 company and now had funds to buy guns, which they mostly used against one another, fighting for territory and even turning brother against brother.

At first, the Professor didn't understand why the government would allow a young black man to become rich, thus making him a threat, but then he realized the answer: the war on drugs. That was not something even the Professor foresaw, but it showed the ripple effect of the powerful drug he had created. The government issued a bill for $1.7 billion to fight crack, $97 million to build new prisons, and $200 million for the construction and staffing of treatment centers because the crack epidemic had spilled into the white communities as well, making them collateral damage. The war on drugs launched police forces around the United States into immediate action, creating special task forces to attack the 'hoods where crack was being sold, and the government even created their own task force, the Drug Enforcement Agency (DEA), to take down the few dealers who were far too big and powerful for the 'hood. Law enforcement quickly slammed their iron fists, attacking 'hood by 'hood, showing no mercy. Drug case after drug case flooded the courtrooms, and prisons were filled beyond capacity with young blacks and Latinos, whose communities were the worst affected by crack cocaine epidemic. Even though the numbers for crack-related arrests were staggering, the police couldn't even make a scratch in the crack game. For every dealer they took down, ten more took his place. The Professor knew the government had planned it that way. He was convinced that it was never about stopping drugs, especially since the government was making so much money off of everything to do with crack—from the seizure of drug money, to a cutthroat court system where your chances of beating your case depended on how much money you had, to a prison they had built to lock drug offenders up for years at a time, renting out bed space like it was a Holiday Inn. Even when the drug offender got out, nobody was going to hire a felon, meaning he was likely to turn back to drugs to support himself, which only started the vicious cycle all over again. The government now had the only recession-proof business in the world, and black and Latino people were there pawns.

The Professor had seen enough, so he spent his spare time working on the drug he had never had the chance to show to the government before they had fired him. He was, in essence, planning his revenge. In the meantime, he warned people about different medications he didn't trust, and he gave out prescriptions to people who couldn't afford them, helping out his people by any means. It wasn't till he started coming to work drunk, denying people flu shots because he said it was poisoning the children, that he got fired from the clinic where he worked. After he lost his medical license, the Professor then turned his focus fully on his new drug. Like a dope fiend with a crack addiction, the Professor searched day and night for his high, which he knew would only come from the completion of his drug. The Professor finally chased his high down. Not only did he complete the drug, but he made it even better than he had planned back when he was younger.

The K-9 drug potency level was off the charts; users could take crack and heroine at the same, with a chaser of crystal meth, but K-9 was still far more potent. The professor also made the drug from cheap household products that wouldn't be easy to trace, cutting costs and keeping his movement under the radar. Once he whipped the chemicals together the way he did, it was impossible to break the K-9 down to see what it was made of, so no one could duplicate it or stop it. The only one who had the antidote was him; he had no choice but to create it, because he had to test the drug on himself to master it. The only bad part was, by the time the Professor finished completing his drug, he was low on funds, and his drinking had caught up with him.

There was no way he could afford to release his drug on his own, so he thought of a plan. He started treating patients out of his home, mostly criminals who couldn't risk going to the hospital. All he had to do was find the right person to fund him. The only problem was that he was always drunk, and when he told people about his super-drug, he knew he probably sounded just like a drunken old fool. It wasn't until the night when King came in with his brother Red on his shoulder, dying from a shotgun wound, with three-year-old No'fere holding on to his pant leg that all that changed. The Professor had heard of King, a legend in the streets who had the love of his whole 'hood like he was the leader, even though he sold drugs to them. The Professor decided that was his chance, and he put it all on the table to King as they waited for Red to recover. The Professor told King everything, from how he'd help to create crack and possibly AIDS, to a new drug that could take over. He assured King he knew how they could do it. The Professor was nervous at first about telling all his secrets, but he had nothing to lose and all his people to save. Even though the alcohol was dripping from every word he spoke, King heard the truth in the man's story; to make sure he did, the Professor showed him the drug in action.

Now, almost twenty-three years later, he was on the verge of seeing his plan finally executed. The Professor had been deep in thought, but the strong, sweet grape smell of purple kryptonite snapped him back to reality.

While the Professor was caught in his daydream, No'fere and Tish had sneaked off with their duffle bags of the purple kryptonite. No'fere had rolled some of it up and lit it.

"Hey!" the Professor yelled to No'fere and Tish, like he was trying to stop them.

"Deuces, Professor!" they both yelled back.

The Professor just shook his head and laughed. He was planning to give them the weed anyhow.

* * *

As they exited the warehouse, getting ready to leave and go enjoy the night, they could hear the approaching motor of Red's black '69 Cutlass as it raced up the long dirt road, heading toward the warehouses. Within seconds, he had pulled up, and he and his passenger were exiting the vehicle as No'fere and Tish loaded their black duffle bags full of marijuana into the trunk of Tish's white '85 Cutlass, with powder-white interior. When they saw the look on Red's face as he approached, they knew something wasn't right.

He quickly started speaking, proving their suspicions right. "Tish, No'fere, we got a problem!" Red said to his niece and his son.

"What's happening, Pops?" No'fere asked, anxiously wanting an answer.

"The appeal for King hasn't gone through. We kidnapped Junior too soon!"

"So what do we do now?" Tish quickly asked, becoming angered at the thought of not getting the chance to finally see her father.

"Nothing. All we can do is wait. I need y'all to lie low from here on out, until I get to the bottom of what's going on," Red said, mad as hell on the inside and feeling like he'd been fucked over. Just to get an appeal for King was going to take an extra $5 million, on top of the $2 million he'd already paid to the crooked federal attorney, Hatcher. Red had paid the man weeks ago and was told that he'd be given an appeal date for King in the next couple months. At that point, he'd immediately set his and King's plan into. Today, though, he'd received a phone call from Hatcher demanding $5 million more. He had gone to look for Hatcher to settle that little disagreement, but there was no sign of the federal attorney anywhere. Now Red knew he had no choice but to make everybody lie low till he could find Hatcher, who had mysteriously taken a leave of absence from work. *He can't hide forever,* Red thought to himself, right before he snatched the blunt out of No'fere's hands.

"Damn, Pops!" No'fere said. He hated when his pops caught him slipping, which Red seemed to take pride in doing every chance he got.

"Shut up, sucka," Red said, hitting the weed and almost coughing his lungs out as the purple kryptonite filled his lungs.

Tish just laughed at the two of them, but as she looked across the parking lot at Red's passenger, who was still sitting on the car, she knew somebody wasn't going to be laughing when the two of them caught up with them.

"Stay out of trouble, ya dig?" Red said as he turned and walked off, still smoking the blunt he had snatched from his son. He knew when it came to Tish and No'fere staying out of trouble, that wasn't an easy task, so he thought he ought to remind them.

Minutes later, Tish and No'fere sped off in the white Cutlass, leaving Red with his friend Sam, who had slid off the car so he could get the blunt from Red as he passed it.

Sam stood six-six and weighed 250 pounds. He had dark brown skin, pork chop sideburns, and a big afro that made him look like he was straight out of a seventies black gangsta movie. He was dressed all in black, including his black U.S. Army jacket that he wore with pride. He stood there next to Red, smoking the blunt, and asked, "What's the deal, Red?"

"We about to go find this muthafucka!" Red said back, giving his man a knuckle-to-knuckle dap.

"I can dig it," Sam replied. He didn't care what Red needed, as he would ride or die for King or Red. If it hadn't been for the two brothers, he knew he'd probably be doing life. He couldn't do nothing but shake his head as he took another hit of the reefah, thinking back on what he'd been through.

* * *

Sam's mother was a prostitute, and there wasn't no telling which one of her johns was his father, so he spent most of his early childhood watching a revolving door of men. The sound of his mother's headboard banging against the wall in their one-bedroom, roach-infested apartment was a common occurrence. Then one cold winter night, when Sam was only six, there was a new sound: gunfire. One of her regular johns pulled out a .38 revolver and shot his mother three times in the face, then turned the gun on himself and blew his brains out. When the police arrived, they found little Sam, covered in blood, holding his mom's dead body and trying to wake her up.

Because the boy had no known family, he ended up living with one foster family after the next. Some thought he was retarded, because after the night his mother died, he refused to talk. Ten years after her death and thirty foster homes later, he was placed in a foster home that would change his life. That family, a white family, was the Petersons. They had seven foster kids, and all of them were black. They were also females, all except for Sam. He remembered thinking, when he met the Petersons for the first time, that they looked like something out of a traveling circus. Ma Peterson was six-two, 230 pounds, and wore way too much makeup, which made her look like a clown.

Pa Peterson was five-six, 130 pounds, with a bald head on top and hair going around the sides. They were some of the nicest foster parents Sam had ever met. After his first month there, he was hoping he would never have to go anywhere else. The girls had to share two rooms, but for the first time in his life, Sam had his very space.

The only problem he had was making friends in the rough neighborhood, especially considering he didn't talk. A lot of kids bullied him, but two brothers, up-and-coming drug dealers named Red and King, always stuck up for him, and once people saw that he was hanging with them, they left him alone.

After Sam spent his long days running behind Red and King, Ma Peterson always came and tucked him in at night. She always brought him warm milk, and for some reason, every time he drank it, he fell right to sleep and didn't hear a sound all night. One night, Ma Peterson followed her normal routine and came in with the milk. She tucked him in and put his milk on the nightstand.

When she left the room, Sam reached for his glass and knocked it over by accident. To his surprise, he saw half-dissolved pills in the bottom of the glass. Sam didn't know what to do at first or what to think; he was definitely in denial, as it was obvious she'd been drugging him for the whole time, but the real question that drove him crazy for the next hour was why. Sam heard footsteps approaching, and he quickly pretended to be asleep.

"Yeah, he sleeping like a baby, Ma," Pa Peterson yelled

downstairs to Ma Peterson. Then the room door closed again.

Sam listened as the footsteps went back down the hallway, then he quickly and quietly jumped out of bed, grabbed his doorknob, and turned it as slowly as he could, trying not to make a sound. When he opened the door, the hallway was dark except for the light shining from underneath the girls' room doors and the light coming from downstairs, where Ma Peterson was. Sam tiptoed down the hallway, past the stairs, hoping Ma Peterson wouldn't see him as he went by.

As he approached the first bedroom, he knelt down and looked through the lock hole in the door. He could see that all the girls in the room were crying, but he noticed one was missing. Suddenly, he was started by the scream of a little girl, coming from the next room, almost causing him to fall down. He regained his balance and made his way toward the next room. In his mind, he wanted to deny this was happening, but the banging of the headboard was a sound he knew all too well. Sam nervously looked through the lock hole on the second bedroom, and his suspicions proved to be true. He could see Pa Peterson with his pants around his ankles, humping like a dog in heat, as the twelve-year-old black girl screamed for him to stop. Sam went in to the bathroom across the hall from the room. The nervousness that had filled his body only moments ago had now turned to rage. He went under the bathroom sink and grabbed the big, red, rusty monkey wrench that Pa

Peterson always used to tighten up the pipe when it leaked. By that time, Pa Peterson had started anally raping the little girl, and her screams seemed to ring through Sam's soul as he approached the door, gripping the monkey wrench tightly in his right hand. Grabbing the doorknob with his left hand, he opened it quickly, but Mr. Peterson was so caught up in raping the girl that he never even heard Sam approach till it was too late. Sam was about three feet away when the old floor made a creaking sound.

Pa Peterson quickly pulled himself out of the girl and turned around, only to see Sam standing there. "Look, boy, you take your ass back to your room now, 'fore you get a whippin' you won't forget." he said in his redneck accent.

"Fück you!" were the first words Sam had said in ten years.

The sound of those words sent a chill down Pa Peterson's spine. All along, he'd thought Sam was a retard, but now he could see that something had definitely changed. "She wanted this!" Peterson said, trying to convince Sam, but those were the last words he would ever say.

Sam brought the monkey wrench crashing down on the side of his head. The first blow came with so much force that Peterson's neck broke, sending him falling to the floor. Blood poured out the side of his head, but Sam was in a rage and continued to beat the man over and over, till he crushed every bone in his face. When he finally stopped, Sam couldn't believe what he'd just done. The blood covered both his hands, there was blood splattered all over his face, and his heart was beating 100 miles an hour.

The little girl was in shock but was relieved she had been saved as she watched her blood-covered hero walk out of the room, on his way to pay the rapist's wife a visit. Ma Peterson knew her husband liked fucking little black girls, but she didn't care, so long as he didn't leave her. The only reason they'd taken Sam in in the first place was so people wouldn't get suspicious of what was going on. Ma Peterson was in the kitchen, finishing up the dishes, when she heard footsteps approaching. "Pa, you done already?" she said, not even turning around as she continued to wash a plate.

"Yeah, bitch, he done!" Sam whispered in her ear.

Ma Peterson was paralyzed with fear, and the plate she was washing fell to the floor and shattered into pieces, just like her nasty husband's face.

"What's wrong? I just want another glass of milk, Ma," Sam lied, right before he wrapped his belt around his neck to strangle her. Ma Peterson was big, but she was no match for Sam's strength. He lifted her off her feet, gripping the belt so tightly that he didn't know if it was his blood or Pa Peterson's dripping from his hands. He refused to let go till every breath in her body was gone.

That night, Sam left and never went back. He knew police would be looking for him, so he did the first thing that came to mind: He went to a heroine spot where Red and King were working out of the Marion Jones projects. When Sam showed up at the door, covered in blood,

King answered and quickly took him in.

"What happened?" Red asked, knowing the little man probably wouldn't answer him because he never spoke. But to Red's and King's surprise, this time Sam had an answer.

"I killed them!"

Red's and King's young minds knew they had to help their friend out, and King quickly jumped into action. Twenty-four hours later, King had gotten Sam a bogus I.D. with a fake name, claiming that the boy was eighteen. All Sam had to do was join the Army, for it was the only place he could disappear.

The U.S. Army quickly accepted Sam, even though his I.D. said he was five-seven, but he was really six-three. He was pretty sure he could have told him he was sixteen, and they still would have enlisted him, as the Army was quick to take any black man who would be willing to go to Vietnam.. Three months of basic training was all he received. That was three months shy of the six-month requirement, but with the war at its peak, it was the best they could do.

Bloodshed was all Sam saw for the next two years of his life, and the smell of death woke him up every morning like a hot cup of coffee. Some soldiers weren't cut out for war, and all they wanted to do was go home, but as far as Sam was concerned, the combat zone was home, and he embraced every second of it. By the time the war was over, Sam had killed well over sixty people and mastered everything from explosives to hand-to-hand combat to every gun you could think of. Everybody in the platoon was scared of him, as killing just came to natural to him.

After the Vietnam war was over, Sam just kept reenlisting in the Army, and he was a Special Forces operative for twenty-plus years. He was honorably discharged after receiving almost every medal the Army had to offer. His only problem then was where he was going to go. He had no family, and as for the only friends he had in his life, he didn't know if they were dead or alive. Unfortunately for him, he made his decision too late; by the time he came home and found Red, King was already in prison. Sam took that personally, considering he felt like he owed them. So, for the next ten years, Sam taught Tish, No'fere, and Red how to kill and survive in the jungle, just like the Army had taught him.

* * *

"Let's go make sure these kids ain't killed everybody," Red said, breaking Sam's train of thought.

"Hell, yeah," Sam quickly agreed, knowing his pupils, No'fere and Tish, too well. He just shook his head as he and Red walked off to see the aftermath of Tish's and No'fere's interrogation.

* * *

The house where Tish and No'fere laid their heads was about twenty minutes away, but Tish managed to get there in ten.

"Damn! You got a date?" No'fere asked as Tish pulled up in front of their house.

"You so nosy," she replied.

"Whatever," No'fere said, looking his cousin in her eyes, like he could see into her soul, before he got of out the car and took the bags of marijuana out of the trunk.

"Don't wait up," Tish said out the window, laughing as she pulled off from the curb.

No'fere knew where his cousin, whom he treated like his little sister, was headed. He had seen that look in her eyes before, not to mention he had been following her to keep her safe from herself. No'fere would've usually jumped in his black BMW 745 and followed her, but tonight he just let her go, not knowing that his decision would come back to haunt him later. No'fere had business to tend to that he took great pleasure in doing.

He entered their four-bedroom house with the duffle bags of weed in his hands. He wasted no time rolling up another Blackwood cigar full of the purple kryptonite he had gotten from the Professor, considering his father had stolen the blunt he'd been smoking at the warehouse. No'fere loved smoking, but he didn't love it nearly as much as counting money. Within a few minutes of lighting his blunt, he had made his way to the hallway closet and dragged four duffle bags across the living room, filled with money. No'fere poured the money out of the bags onto the floor next to him as he took a seat on the long black leather couch in front of the glass coffee table with the money counter on it. No'fere turned the channel of the big-screen TV to Sportscenter as the blunt hung out of his lips. He quickly put down the remote, then sat there in his wife-beater and picked up a handful of money. He started feeding the money counter like it was a buffet. He was about $200,000 in when he heard a sound from behind, causing him to quickly jump up and spin around with his .45 automatic in his hand, taking aim toward the darkness of the kitchen.

* * *

It had been an hour since Tish had dropped No'fere off and put her Cutlass in her garage at her house on the lake, the one she'd been keeping secret from everybody—or so she thought. Tish had dressed quickly, changing from her pink wig to a long, straight black one to match the back mini-skirt, black eyeliner, and black leather boots that climbed up to her knees. She hated that her chance to finally see her family had been postponed. Even though she used the house as a hideout, she made sure it had two extra bedrooms, hoping the twin brothers she'd never met would get the chance to stay there one day.

Tish didn't hold bad blood toward her parents for letting her believe her aunt was her mother all those years. Living her life not knowing who she was had been the story of her life, and she had gotten used to it over the years. Even after finding out about who she really was, she'd had to take on the identity of Aisha Taylor in order to stay hidden and be able to take a role in her father's bigger plan, the one her Uncle Red had told her pieces of; he always kept everyone on a need-to-know basis.

Tish had built Aisha's credibility and background by running Club Redlight with her cousin No'fere and selling high-grade marijuana to high-end clients only. She knew selling to high-end clients meant more money and more safety; anybody with a lot to lose didn't want the whole world knowing that all day, they'd been performing heart surgeries, but when they got off work, they were selling hundreds of pounds of marijuana to their friends and colleagues. She gave them privacy and top-grade product, and they gave her money and any favor she needed—and she never hesitated asking for one. She had just gotten some pills from one of her clients, a psychiatrist, after she'd told him she had a friend with a personality disorder who didn't know who she was at times.

She stood in the bathroom in her house, looking in the mirror to make sure she was looking awesome as usual. She looked down at the pills in the brown bottle with the white top. Her client had told her they'd help with what he thought sounded like a case of mild schizophrenia. Tish just shook her head in disgust and quickly threw them down in the sink, refusing to take a pill like she was sick. She stood there with her head down, her long black hair covering her face, wrestling with the voices in her head. *Tish, take the pill! Your uncle said we've got to lie low and stay out of trouble,* one voice said, but the other screamed, *Aisha, it's time to play! Take the pill tomorrow.* She slowly raised head. Her brown eye peeking through her hair as she looked at her reflection again in the mirror. She then flipped her straight razor out in front of her face like it was a switchblade. Her eyes found their reflection in the shiny blade. It was the same straight razor Larry had used to keep her in check while he raped her, back when she was younger. After she killed him, she took it from his dead body, before her uncle disposed of it. She began grinning as she felt her pussy start pulsating and becoming wet from her excitement, making her let out a slight moan of pleasure. "Yeah, just one more night!" she whispered out loud after moaning. Then she let out a devilish giggle that even she didn't recognize.

Within minutes, one of her two garage doors opened, and she pulled out of the garage in a white Benz, personalized with her Aisha license plates.

Within fifteen minutes, the bright lights of the uppity nightclub, Studio Nine, filled the cold midnight air.

"You belong to me now, bitch!" she said, thinking out loud as she went to park, knowing her target was right inside the club. She was so excited she didn't even realize her hand was inside her panties, exploring her wetness.

* * *

As No'fere stood there holding his pistol with both hands, his finger caressing the hairpin trigger, the darkness of the kitchen now had a sound he knew all too well: the sound of high-heeled shoes walking across the kitchen floor in his direction. No'fere just remained calm and almost cracked a smile as he waited patiently for his visitor to emerge. Within seconds, the sound of the high heels had a face to go with it. *And a sexy one at that,* No'fere thought to himself as he found himself staring at Head District Attorney Ramos, who was now standing in his living room.

"Gun charge, five years. Weed possession..." she said, pausing to kick one of the open duffle bags of purple kryptonite before continuing. "Twenty years. Put that with all that money on the floor, and let's just say I can round your time off to natural life!" she finished in her Mexican accent. She was dressed in a tan business suit top, a white blouse that showed her cleavage, and a tan business skirt that wore her very well.

No'fere just snickered under his breath and kept his aim on his target as she began walking around the couch.

"That's a lot of time," she began to say, pulling the hairclip off the back of her hair, releasing her long black mane down her back as she made her way around the couch till she was face to face with the gun and its owner. "Maybe if you have something for me, I might just be able to look the other way, but you better make it good, 'cause I already got enough on you and your cousin to push forward with my case."

No'fere just looked over his shoulder at all the money on the floor. Even though he had been running the money through the money counter earlier, he had counted so much money over the years that he knew just by looking at it that it was about a million dollars, give or take a few. He turned back around and stated talking. "How about I fuck you on top of a million dollars?" he said with a straight face, looking back in the eyes of Ms. Ramos.

"Wow! I go out of my way to come down here and try and help you, and that's the best offer you can come up with? Hmm. Well, I guess if that's all you've got to offer, I'm going to have to take what I can get, considering I don't feel like doing all that paperwork anyway," she said.

No'fere threw the pistol on the couch and took Ms. Ramos in his arms, lifting her up off her feet. Her legs quickly wrapped around his waist. Their lips met, and their tongues passionately became acquainted. Her hands gripped his rock-solid arms that held her with ease, and he carried her to the pile of money and dropped to his knees, laying her softly on top of it. He sat back to open his pants, but she sat up with her legs spread and pulled his dick out for him. She lay back down, pulling her cream-colored Victoria's Secret lace boy shorts to the side, displaying her juice box. No'fere paused only for a second as she tasted her sweet juices off her fingers, and then he pushed his dick deep inside her, till she felt it in her stomach. His aggressive nature only added fuel to her fire that was already burning between her thighs, and she grabbed him and pulled him in deeper, finding pleasure in the pain. No'fere pumped harder and harder, till the screams off "Papi! Oh, papi!" filled the air as she dug her nails in. He felt her body begin to orgasm viciously, releasing all her pleasure on the dick that he just kept pounding inside her.

"Oh, papi, fuck me!" she screamed out, making him fuck her harder and harder till she felt the pressure build up in his dick. Right before it was ready to explode his seed all up inside her, she quickly pulled it out and sat up. She put No'fere's dick in her mouth and sucked all the cum out, then licked up the extras. Five minutes, later Ms. Ramos was coming out of the bathroom after freshening up after her sexual encounter.

No'fere was standing in front of the TV, looking at the game he'd turned to, with a blunt hanging from his lips. He had no problem smoking in her presence. He looked back at her as she wrapped her long hair back up. "You know I could've shot your ass !"

"I know, but who gon' shoot somebody as sexy as me?" she responded.

No'fere just shook his head, remembering the first time he'd met her.

* * *

It was one of the coldest days of the year in the City of Vision as the frail, fourteen-year-old No'fere made his way through the streets. The bitter cold air caused a numbness in his light-skinned face, which could barely be seen from up under his black hood. *If I hurry and make these pickups,* I can get my ass home and out of this cold, he thought. He had made his first pickups for his father Red, and there was only one left, at a jewelry store on the upper-class side of town, and it was his first time to make that particular pickup.

When he approached the store and pulled on the door, he was surprised to find that it didn't come open, especially considering he could see a couple people inside. "What the fuck?" he said, thinking out loud. He had already been punished by the cold air enough, and he definitely didn't want to get home and be punished by Red as well. The buzzing sound coming from the door quickly broke his thoughts, and when he pulled on the handle this time, the door came right open. No'fere wasted no time stepping inside and embracing the heat.

He had never been in any jewelry store before, and all the diamonds sparkling in the glass cases quickly caught his eye. He almost didn't hear the little bald-headed Mexican man with the round glasses speaking to him from behind the counter.

"Welcome, my friend. You must be Red's little boy, No'fere?"

"Yep!" No'fere responded quickly, nodding his head from under his hood.

"Well, let me finish with these customers, and I'll be right over to take care of you!" he said, referring to the two white guys who were looking at some diamond watches. Mr. Ramos quickly turned toward the back room and began calling his eighteen-year-old daughter. "Michelle! Michelle!"

Within seconds, the finest girl No'fere had ever seen emerged from the back. She looked black, but her long, straight hair that hung down to the middle of her back, along with her Spanish eyes, let him know she had to be mixed. "Yes, Daddy?" the girl said as she approached her father, proving No'fere's intuition right .

"I would like you to meet No'fere. No'fere, this is my daughter Michelle," Mr. Ramos introduced.

"It's nice to meet you," No'fere said politely, pulling his hood off and displaying the 360 waves he spent hours brushing daily.

His light-skinned complexion definitely caught her attention. "It's nice to meet you too!" Michelle replied, trying to hold back her smile.

"Take our friend in the back, Michelle. I'll be back there in a minute," Mr. Ramos said to his daughter before going back to his waiting customers.

"Right this way," Michelle said, leading No'fere to the back.

No'fere definitely didn't mind following her, as he enjoyed the view of her hips in the tight jeans she was wearing. When they entered the back of the store, No'fere couldn't believe his eyes. The place looked like a luxury crib, complete with big leather sofas, big TVs, and a full bar, like they were in some kind of club. "Damn!" No'fere said, thinking out loud. "Y'all living good." He continued following Michelle to the big black leather couch and took a seat.

"Would you like some lemonade? I made it myself," Michelle offered.

"Yeah, I'll take some," No'fere replied. He couldn't help but stare as Michelle walked off toward the fridge.

She knew exactly what she was doing and put a little extra sway in her walk to make sure she had his full attention. "It's not polite to stare," Michelle said, as if she had eyes in the back of her head.

"It's not polite to tell people it's not polite to stare!" No'fere quickly snapped back.

That caused Michelle to laugh. She was definitely feeling No'fere already. She even put a lemon on his glass, doing her best to impress him. As she returned with his drink, he stood up to get his glass from her, and they seemed to freeze as his hand covered hers on the glass. She couldn't help but look up at No'fere, and they quickly got lost in each other's eyes, as if nothing else in the room even existed.

No'fere couldn't resist her beauty, and he found himself coming in closer and closer, till their lips were inches apart. The fireworks were definitely about to pop off, but unfortunately, that wasn't the only popping going on.

Their attention was quickly was turned toward the loud popping sound that was coming from the other room. No'fere knew it was the sound of gunfire, and his thoughts quickly came to life as the back room door came open. In walked Mr. Ramos, holding his shoulder from a gunshot wound, and right behind him were the two white guys whom No'fere had seen shopping in the store when he'd came in.

"Daaaaaaaaady!" Michelle screamed as the lemonade glass and her father fell to the floor simultaneously. Michelle didn't care about the two gun-wielding white guys as she ran across the room to her father's side.

"Where is the coke, old man!" the blond-haired white guy demanded before kicking Mr. Ramos violently in the head.

"I-I don't know what you're talking about!" Mr. Ramos responded the best he could.

No'fere couldn't believe that shit was going on as he stood there with his hands up. trying to remain calm, knowing he had at least $50 thousand of Red's money in his book bag.

The dark-haired man quickly grabbed Michelle by her long hair and snatched her off the floor, then put his 9mm pistol to her head before he began talking with a Italian accent. "We're not going to ask you again!"

Mr. Ramos wasn't worried about dying, but he definitely didn't want his daughter dead, so he quickly complied. "Okay, okay, it's in the fridge! Just let my daughter go!" he pleaded.

The blond-haired man began laughing before he spoke. "Now that you've told us where the shit is, there's no point in letting any of you live, you stupid old man!" Then he raised his TEC-9, taking aim at Mr. Ramos. He turned and looked at Michelle, who was struggling to get free from the dark-haired man's grasp. "Any last words for your father?" he said, smiling at his partner, who finally had something to say.

"Yeah, bitch. You got something you wanna say before we kill—"

But he never got the chance before a .357 bullet ripped into his forehead, sending skull and brain matter all over the wall behind him and all over Michelle.

The blond man couldn't believe what he was seeing, and his body seemed to go in slow motion as he turned toward No'fere, who was now standing, there holding a snub-nose .357 with the barrel still smoking. "You fucking nigger!" the blond man said. He attempted to turn the TEC-9 on No'fere, but he was no match for No'fere's speed or aim.

No'fere quickly squeezed off two more rounds. The first one caught the blond-haired man in his neck, and the other bullet landed right in the middle of the man's forehead ,damn near decapitating him on the spot.

Michelle quickly made her way back to her father's side, disregarding the blood and brain matter that was covering her. "Daddy? Daddy, are you okay?" she said.

"Yes, baby. Hurry! Help me up," Mr. Ramos responded, knowing he had to move quickly. He had hit the silent alarm and knew it would only be a matter of time before police were swarming like bees on honey. "Quickly, Michelle. Get the stuff out of the stash and give it to No'fere," Mr. Ramos said, holding his shoulder. The burn from the bullet wound was becoming more and more excruciating by the second.

No'fere watched as Michelle came back to the same couch he'd just been sitting on and lifted the couch cushions. To his surprise, there was a wooden door. When Michelle lifted the door, beneath it were two black duffle bags, each containing ten kilos. No'fere was so amazed by the stash spot that he almost didn't hear Mr. Ramos approach.

"No'fere, thank you, my young friend. I owe you my life. Please take these two bags as a token of my gratitude. Let me take care of everything here." Mr. Ramos said, reaching his hand out for No'fere to hand him the gun he was holding. "We must hurry. Tell Red I'll be in touch real soon!"

No'fere wasted no time in wiping his prints off the gun with his shirt and passing it to Mr. Ramos. "Which way should I leave?" No'fere asked as he quickly grabbed the two black bags out of the hiding place in the couch. He knew it was time to get out of there, especially since he could hear the sound of police sirens fast approaching.

"Come on! Hurry out the back!" Michelle said, grabbing No'fere by his arm and leading him toward the back door. She quickly unlocked the locks and pushed the door open for him, but before he could walk out into the cold night air, she grabbed him by his coat with both her hands, like she was jacking him up, pulled him down to her and kissed him deep and passionately on the lips. Before he stood back up, she pulled his hood up on his head for him, realizing his hands were full. "Thank you, No'fere. Now go!" she said, rushing him out the door into the night.

* * *

Ever since that night, she'd been No'fere's main girl. Even when she decided to go to law school, No'fere had happily stood behind her because she had put herself in a position in life to help the movement. A woman like that was someone No'fere couldn't do nothing but love, and he knew she felt the same. even though she was staring at him with an evil look on her face as she approached him, breaking his train of thought.

"You thinking 'bout them other hoes, Fere?" she said to him before she hit him in his chest, making him laugh.

"Naw, baby!" he replied, dodging her next punch.

"Naw, baby, you ain't thinking 'bout your other hoes, or naw you ain't got no other hoes, Fere?" she asked, throwing a trick question out there, followed by another punch.

He caught that one and pulled her into his embrace, calming her down. "Come here, mami. You know I love you and only you!" he said, kissing her quickly on the lips, even though they both knew damn well that he'd managed to avoid answering the question. His second, softer kiss made her retreat.

No'fere was the finest nigga she knew, and there was hoes throwing pussy at him left and right that she knew for a fact he had no problem catching. She had gotten used to it over the years and had learned to just accept him for who he was. *No'fere's a bad boy, but he's my bad boy, and he ain't going nowhere,* she thought to herself. She was never even mad at him in the first place; she just wanted to keep him on his Ps and Qs.

"You'd better get out of here before someone sees you sneaking out the house of a criminal!" No'fere said, laughing.

"Whatever. You just trying to get rid of me. You probably got hoes waiting upstairs for me to leave. You bitches can come out now! I'm leavin', hoes!" she said, walking away like she was angry again. Still, she never wanted to leave his side, especially since No'fere had told her about his role in his family's plan—a role that would put his life and their future together in her hands.

"I love you too," No'fere yelled as his girl walked out the door she had come in and slammed it behind her. He just shook his head, smiling.

"I sure do love your crazy ass, ol' big bootie-ass girl," he said, thinking out loud. He loved to see her pretty face, but he also loved to watch that ass of hers as she walked away.

* * *

Studio Nine was in full swing as Tish made her way across the bar as the sound of techno blasted through the speakers. Blacks and whites, mixed together like salt and pepper, almost filled the huge club to capacity. The club had more drugs in it than a pharmacy, and that—along with beautiful women and expensive drinks—kept it packed and full of high rollers. Tish had only been there ten minutes before she squeezed in at the bar next to a dark-haired white man who was trying to order a drink.

"*Rémy* XO and Sprite!" Tish said, cutting the man off before he could order his drink. When the bartender quickly disappeared to retrieve her drink, she giggled at the man who didn't get his.

"Very assertive. I like that," the man said, laughing as he brushed his white $10,000 suit off before extending his hand and introducing himself. "Kyle Bourgers is the name, and sex is my game," he said, giving his million-dollar smile as he looked her up and down, loving every inch of what he was seeing. He knew right away that he could make her a star.

"The name is Aisha, and thanks for the drink!" she responded, grabbing her drink off the bar and walking away, leaving him with a $100 per glass bill.

He only hesitated to pay because he was busy staring at her ass, thinking about the pain he could cause her. He had to calm his hunger down; his dick was getting too hard too fast. "Another time, another place!" he said, licking his lips as he turned around and threw $100 on the bar.

It was 3 a.m. when Studio Nine let out, but Kyle Bourgers always waited till everybody was almost gone before he left. He liked looking for stragglers to take home to introduce to his life, either for business or his own personal pleasure. The parking lot was almost empty as he came out the back door of Studio Nine, and what he saw stopped him dead in his tracks. The side of his candy apple-red Porsche

911 had been keyed with the word "bitch," and all four tires were flat. He was angry for a second, but he knew there was no use trying to figure out which one of the thousands of females he dealt with for a living had done it. Besides, money didn't mean a thing to Mr. Bourgers. It was the first time he'd driven that car, and it would probably be his last, since he had a whole fleet of them. After all, he'd inherited his father's muti-million-dollar porn business when he was eighteen, after his father and mother were found stabbed to death in their sleep. That was twenty years ago, and now Mr. Bourgers ran his family business relentlessly. He was estimated to be worth $400 million, and that number was climbing daily. "Fuck!" he said, thinking out loud and realizing his cell phone wasn't in his pocket as he searched for it to call a ride. He had just turned to walk back toward the club back door when he heard a car approaching from behind him, causing him to turn around.

"You need a drink?" Tish said from the passenger side window. She was sitting in the driver seat of her Benz, with a bottle of Cristal champagne in her hand.

"I think I will!" he said, feeling instant excitement as he saw who it was that was offering him a ride. He wasted no time getting in the passenger seat.

"This one's on me," she said, passing him the bottle.

He quickly grabbed it and put it to his lips and began drinking. *Cristal now and your blood later,* he thought to himself.

"Where to?" she asked.

"My place," he replied, ready to guide her to his playground.

Twenty minutes later, they pulled down a long, dark road that went through a forest. At the end of the road was an eight-bedroom mini-mansion. It wasn't the one where he lived, but he kept his Barbie dolls there. *And tonight I'm gonna add to my collection,* he thought to himself, as he quickly invited the sexy female he only knew as Aisha inside. The living room was full of expensive white furniture, but the rest of the house looked like a photo studio, full of bright lights and cameras. He quickly went to his massive bar. He walked behind it and grabbed a controller. When he hit a button, the house came alive. A big-screen TV came out of the floor, stadium sound quality techno music came blasting through speakers that couldn't even be seen, just like at the club. "XO and Sprite, right?" he said, grabbing the bottle a *Rémy* XO from his top shelf. He began pouring his guest a drink, making sure he didn't let her see him drop a pill in it—one that would paralyze her and incapacitate her. "How do you like my home?" he asked, passing her the drink he'd made for her.

"I love it!" she said, as she waited for him to come from behind the bar and guide her toward the couch. "This is a lot of liquor. You mind if I smoke?" she said, pulling a joint out of her purse and lighting it up before he could even answer.

"Of course not! Enjoy yourself," he said, still sipping on the bottle of Cristal she'd given him in her car. He knew it would take a while for the effects of the drug he had put in her drink to kick in, and he figured he might as well enjoy himself in the meantime. The sweet smell of the reefah she'd lit up quickly enticed him to take a couple pulls. He hadn't smoked reefah in a while. *This is some serious stuff,* he thought to himself, zoning out as he started feel his body become numb.

"Kyle! Kyle, you okay?" she asked him as he sat back on the couch, trying to pull his thoughts together.

"I'm good," he lied. He was way too high, and he closed his eyes for a second, unable to feel his face or the rest of his body. His mind was racing, trying to figure out what was wrong with him and to remember what all he'd had to drink. His mind didn't have to work that hard on that, though, considering he'd never even gotten his drink at the club. The only thing he'd drank was the bottle of Cristal that Aisha, his chosen victim for the night, had given him earlier. His mind quickly thought about the drug he had been using on his victims, and he tried to remember how long it had been since he'd started drinking, but his fuzzy thoughts were broken by a whisper in his ear.

"I think I'll pass on this drink you made for me. I'm not really that thirsty, Kyle the kid killer!"

At first, he recognized the voice as Aisha, but when she said the last four words, she sounded like another person. That sent chills down his spine that he couldn't even feel. He did his best to open his eyes, but he knew it was no use. *All I can do now is wait,* he thought to himself, trying to cope with the fact that he'd been pegged by that female, and now it was him on the other end of his own sick game.

It had been twenty minutes or so since he'd felt his body being dragged across the floor. The drug he had been given had paralyzed him, preventing him from moving, but he could still feel every touch. He was caught off guard by one of his eyelids being forced open; a metal clip was inserted in his eye to hold his eyelid open, leaving him unable to blink. Within seconds, he could see again as the clips held his eyes open painfully. He looked around and knew exactly where he was: in his own doll room—the very room where he took his victims to rape, kill, and dismember them, cutting off their heads, arms, legs. Once he did that, he would surgically sew the body parts to different bodies and leave them for the police to find, making it nearly impossible to identify the victims because they had body parts from four other victims attached. The police and media had dubbed him Mismatch, or "the mismatch killer," and he had been using his business to find his females and hide his secrets ever since he'd beaten his parents to death twenty years earlier; he escaped suspicion by telling the police he hadn't even been there.

Now, facing his own bloody death, he wanted to punish Aisha badly—so badly that his dick got hard as a rock just thinking about it. What he really wanted, though, was to drink her blood. The effects of the drug began to wear off, giving him some movement back. He knew it wouldn't be but a few more minutes before he got all his movement back, but he also knew it would do him no good, for she'd already strapped him to the table he used for his killing procedures, with leather straps around his ankles and wrists. The table was flat, only allowing him to look up at the bright light in the ceiling; the fluorescent beams burned his eyes since he couldn't blink, and he began to go crazy from that alone. Suddenly, the table quickly flipped up, forcing him into an upright position. It took him a second to get his balance, as his jelly-like legs were just getting their movement back, and his vision was still blurry. When his eyes finally cleared a bit, what he saw was like something out of a horror movie.

Across the walls of his special room were thousands of faces of females—all his victims from the past. He was being forced to face his demons, and his mind began to panic as his eyes scanned each and every picture. He began to whisper their names, where he'd met them, and when, and after a while, it was as if he was chanting.

The words of Aisha broke him from his trance-like state. "You're my bitch now!" she said as she came around the side of the table.

He tried his best to turn his neck to look at her. He also tried to speak to her, but as soon as he opened his mouth, he felt the touch of the straight razor slicing into the corner off his mouth, ripping halfway through his flesh and leaving blood pouring out, his jaw wide open. He screamed with pain and struggled to get free, but she didn't care; she just swung the straight razor again, slicing the other side of his mouth, leaving both sides off his face ripped open.

As he screamed she just laughed, but he didn't even recognize her voice anymore; it was as if someone else was in the room with them. "You're my bitch now! You're my bitch now! You're my bitch now!" she said, faster and faster, over and over.

He panicked, realizing she was just as sick as he was. Just as the thought left his mind, she dug her straight razor down his chest, trying to cut through to the bone. The pain was unbearable as his skin peeled open. He just closed his eyes and hoped it would be over soon, but she took her time, making four downward stripes down his chest, then crossing them over with a diagonal line, like she was using hash marks to keep some kind of bloody tally.

He did his best to beg, but the more he tried to talk, the more pain and blood filled his mouth, making it impossible. Then, just when he thought he couldn't feel no greater pain than he'd already felt or get any closer to death, he felt his still-erect dick split open like a polish sausage in boiling water as she ran the razor up his family jewels, right up the tip of his dick. His body jerked and jerked as he screamed louder and louder, only making it harder on himself as the blood poured in a puddle onto the floor. His family jewels now hung outside the skin freely. The pain was almost too much to bear, and he felt himself passing out right before the razor came slashing across his neck from ear to ear. She stuck a $100 bill in his mouth as she watched his bloody body go limp.

Within minutes, she had cleaned herself up and jumped in her car. She was ready to get out of there. She looked back at the mansion one last time, and she could've sworn she saw something in the upstairs window, but she blew it off and pulled off down the dirt road, confused and disorientated. She had no idea why she was there or how she had gotten to that house, and she couldn't remember anything that had happened since she'd dropped No'fere off, but she wasn't about to stick around to find out, especially since the razor on the front seat of her car was covered in blood. She just shook her head as she drove down the road. It wasn't the first time this had happened, but she hoped it might be the last.

PART II

BLOOD OUT

CHAPTER FOUR

You Reap What You Sow

It had been a crazy eight months since U.S. Attorney Hatcher had run off with $2 million of Red's money, the money that was supposed to cover his little brother King's appeal so they could kick their master plan off. Hatcher had taken a sudden leave of absence from work, blaming it on some illness he'd thought up. It didn't matter anyway, because no one was going to question him. He had deep connections to ensure his employment, and he also had $2 million to keep anyone from suggesting otherwise. Hatcher had been partying hard for the last six months, hiding from Red, but as he lay asleep in his condo, passed out from partying with hookers and drinking, he never would've thought that the noise that woke him from his drunken sleep would turn out to be Red, sitting right there in a chair in the corner of his bedroom.

The darkness barely covered Red's face as the light from the window glared on his gold teeth. Hatcher would never forget that gold grin that had almost made his heart jump out of his body the first time he'd met Red, especially because he knew even then that he was about to rip Red off. Hatcher normally didn't do business like that, but he had been told by some dangerous people that he should take the money and disappear and let them take care of the little problem. In this moment, though, as he sat his semi-bald, chunky, pale white frame up in his bed, he had to wonder if he was more scared of the ones who'd given him that advice or of Red, who was now glaring at him from across the room.

"Nice place you have here," Red said in a calm voice that really scared Hatcher.

Hatcher began to try to explain himself, but he was cut off abruptly.

"You and I both know I'm not here to compliment the place you bought with *my* money," Red interrupted, "but then again, I don't actually care about the money." Then, he whistled.

Suddenly, the bedroom door burst open. Hatcher looked toward it and what he saw made his heart stop and left him speechless.

Red just cracked a grin as his boy Sam walked in, wearing all black. He had a green .40-caliber handgun pressed firmly against the forehead of a sandy-haired, skinny white man in his flannel pajamas. The skinny man's words were restricted by the duct tape that covered his mouth, so he just looked at Hatcher with tears in his eyes.

"Patrick!" Hatcher said as he watched the tears of his brother run down his face.

"Yeah, Patrick," Red said, pausing to light the Newport

King he was holding between his lips. "Mr. Hatcher, I thought I should take this time to explain something to you. In this world, there are few I'm willing to die for, but my little brother is one of them. Even though we both share a common factor in life, both of us having a brother, I wonder if we share the same state of mind when it comes to protecting them," Red said, pausing again to blow the Newport smoke out his mouth and leaning back in his chair.

No sooner than Red's back touched the chair than Sam squeezed the trigger of his .40 caliber, splattering the pajama-clad man's blood and brains all over Hatcher's white sheets and him.

"Paaaaaaaatrick!" Hatcher screamed as his older brother's lifeless body fell to the floor before his eyes. Hatcher froze up instantly. His mind went blank. He was so caught up in the moment, watching one of his two brothers die in front of him, that he almost didn't hear Red began talking again.

"You have only one brother remaining, so perhaps we'll see more eye to eye now. I'm sure now you can fully feel the love I have for my only brother, the one you've refused to help," Red said as he got up from his seat and headed toward the room where Sam was waiting. "I hope we don't have to have another family reunion!" Red finished as he walked out the door with Sam. He closed the door behind him, leaving Hatcher in the bed to stare at what was left of his older brother Patrick, who was now a puddle of blood on his bedroom floor.

* * *

It had only been two days since Red and Sam had paid Hatcher a visit and given him the option of losing his younger brother or helping King get his appeal, as he'd been paid to do. *I'm sure this will be a death sentence for me, but I'd rather die than to see my one remaining brother killed over something that's got nothing to do with him,* Hatcher thought to himself as he rapidly packed his clothes and the remaining $500,000 he had from the money Red had given him for King's appeal, which he'd finally managed to push through. Hatcher couldn't do anything now but run, and no sooner than he'd zipped his bag up and checked his pocket for his plane ticket, he was out the door of his condo, making his way downstairs to call for a cab to take him to the airport.

Hatcher was paranoid, knowing death could be lurking around any corner and his eyes quickly saw that there was a new young white doorman working the door. Everything seemed to be going in slow motion as Hatcher approached the doorman except his heart, which was beating so fast he thought it might burst right out of his chest. He wondered if he should just turn around and run, but the doorman's abrupt movement stopped him dead in his tracks. The nervous Hatcher almost dropped his bags as the man began speaking.

"Are you okay, sir? Can I get you cab?" the doorman

asked, seeing the startled look on Hatcher's face.

"No thank you," Hatcher said, knowing he had let his paranoia get the best of him. He was embarrassed about his actions, so he decided to hail his own cab, even though he knew that it was difficult to catch one in the city, even at night. As he stepped out in the night air, he wasted no time looking for a cab. To his surprise, one quickly sped up to greet him, and opened the back door and jumped in. "To the airport!" Hatcher said to the skinny blond-haired white cab driver.

The cabbie didn't do anything but hit the meter and pull off from the curb into traffic.

Hatcher felt a little relief as he sat back in the taxi seat, knowing that in a couple hours, he would be on his way to the Bahamas. He was thinking so hard he almost didn't realize that the cab was not going to the airport. Instead, it had turned off in a warehouse district. "Hey! What the fuck you turning off for? You going to make me miss my flight!" Hatcher said to the driver.

The driver didn't answer. He just closed and locked the little bulletproof security window that separated them and continued to drive.

Hatcher's panic quickly set back in as the cab came to a halt and the driver immediately jumped out and left him in the back. Hatcher reached for the door handles, but he couldn't find any—something he'd overlooked when he'd first gotten in, since he was so eager to get to the airport and fly out of there. *I can't even roll the window down!* he thought to himself, looking out the window.

A heavyset bald white guy with a pale white complexion and a long black trench coat began to approach the car.

"The Reaper!" Hatcher said, thinking out loud, knowing his life was about to end. The Reaper was the most feared hit man in the United States; in fact, Hatcher had used him many times in the past to make some people disappear. Now, there the Reaper was, standing right outside Hatcher's own cab, with a devilish grin on his face. "I hope those black dudes kill you, Agent Fellows," Hatcher said aloud. He knew Fellows had sent the Reaper to get him. Still, his survival instincts kicked in, and he quickly grabbed his money bag. He unzipped it and grabbed up handfuls of cash, ready to buy his way out of the situation.

Unfortunately for Hatcher, when he looked back, he was met by the rapid fire of the AR-15 the Reaper had pulled from under his black coat. The Reaper fired away into the backseat of the cab, the bullets pouring down on Hatcher like a hail storm, making it impossible for him to escape. Hundred-dollar bills filled the air like Magic City on a Monday as twenty bullets filled his body, leaving him slumped against the door with bloody cash in his hands. The Reaper just turned and laughed, then disappeared into the night air.

* * *

As soon as Red received the call from King's lawyer, letting him know the appeal had been pushed through, Red instantly threw their plan into effect. He hoped they could still salvage the original plan, but they didn't have a lot of time to make it happen.

* * *

It was early afternoon, and the fat black bail bondsman everybody knew as Fat Cat sat behind his desk, eating a sloppy double cheeseburger. His two cute young black secretaries wiped the food of his mouth while he chewed, as if he was some kind of king. Fat Cat was more than just a bondsman. He ran numbers, pimped females, and most of all, he was a hit broker. If a person needed somebody dead, Fat Cat was the man to see; if they needed info, he was the man to see; if they needed a snitch bonded out and killed, Fat Cat was definitely the man to see. He took pride in his job and it benefits, and he was so caught up in the benefits at the moment that the bells ringing from the door opening almost made him grab his sawed-off shotgun that was in a holster under his desk. Fortunately, some cruel words eased his mind.

"What up, fatso?" Tish said from behind her black Gucci glasses. Of course she had a big black Gucci purse and an outfit to match.

"Aisha! What's happening, sweetheart!" the fat man said, brushing his females out of the way to greet the female he knew as Aisha.

She saw him struggling to get his big self up out of the chair. "You can stay in your seat. I won't be long," she said.

Tish had known Fat Cat for a while and had used him for info many times. She'd even done a few freelance hits for him from time to time. "What's the price tag for Junior? I got somebody inquiring," she asked.

Fat Cat didn't care who was inquiring. All he ever cared about were dollar signs. "Y'all go play," he said to his two females, sending to them to the back. He knew it was serious talk if it had to do with Junior, who had been missing for the last eight months. Junior already had a heavy price on his head from the Italians, but since his disappearance, his father had put up a $5 million reward for the return of his son. That forced the Italians to match the $5 million offer. It didn't matter who got Junior. Fat Cat knew that either way, it was going to be a big payday for him. "It's $5 million—$3 million for you and $2 million for me," he answered, even though his greedy ass was thinking of a way to get his hands on the whole $10 million.

"Make it happen and call me when they want to meet!" Tish said, and she turned to walk away.

Fat Cat had let the thought of money and her good looks almost cloud his vision, but finally he snapped back to his senses. "Wait…how I know you even got Junior?" he said, stopping Tish in her tracks. When she reached in her purse, he was a bit worried. Fat Cat liked the female he knew as Aisha, but he also knew she was dangerous, and her actions made him lean forward and caress the handle of his sawed-off.

"You know you would never even get a shot off,." she

said like she had eyes in the back of her head, making him let go of the shotgun. She turned around and threw something on his desk. "Is this enough proof?" she asked.

The fat man looked at a human hand lying next to the cheeseburger he was in the middle of devouring. "Damn, Aisha!" he said, jumping back in his seat, almost breaking his chair.

"Call me, okay? And one more thing…keep this between us," she said before she walked out the door, laughing. She knew Fat Cat couldn't keep a secret, especially one that big, and that was exactly what she was counting on.

A black 745 with black tint pulled up to the curb as she exited the bail bonds shop, and she jumped right in the passenger seat.

"What happened?" No'fere asked as he pulled away from the curb.

"It's game time!" Tish responded, lighting the blunt she had rolled in the ash tray.

No'fere was excited ,but he knew that even though his little cousin was dangerous and he would be in the shadows watching over her for a while longer, this was her mission in the master plan both of them had been born into, and his mission depended on hers being successful.

His dad had always preached to him and Tish. He'd often told them, "It's like being part of a basketball team. One of us might be a scorer or a shot blocker, but no matter what position you play, come out and execute your game plan, and everybody around you will do the same. When

G Street Chronicles / 143

it's all said and done, we all have one goal in common, and that's winning the championship."

"Fuck that! I play all positions," No'fere said, thinking out loud as he started grinning.

"I ain't even gonna ask you what you thinking about," Tish said, shaking her head and passing him the blunt.

"What?" he asked, knowing his cousin had caught him thinking too hard and that she always had something smart to say. Soon as he hit the weed, the thought came right back. *Yeah, I'm like the '96 Bulls,* he thought to himself, always so confident, even when death was about to come knocking like the DTs on a 5 a.m. raid.

* * *

Club Redlight had been closed since Junior's bodyguard had been killed in there, but the night of the reopening had arrived, and it seemed like the whole city was there, ready to party. The three-floor, two-dance floor club was in full swing as Tish sat in the soundproof balcony office that looked more like a luxury skybox. She had a fifth of Hennessy XO on the marble table, and she was drinking straight out the bottle, taking long swigs. She was happy Fat Cat had finally called after two weeks and wanted her to come see him the next night. Finally, she was one step closer to the family she'd never known but so desperately wanted to be a part of. She even had plans to take the old black Chevy Caprices to the warehouse and fix them up for her little twin brothers, since Uncle Red had said they'd belonged to her dad. "Yeah, my brothers gon' stay fly just like me," she said, thinking out loud before she took another swig of her Hennessy. She was about to reach in her purse for her Blackwood cigar so she could roll up when a knock at the door caught her attention. Tish looked at one of her security guards at the door and quickly motioned for the big black man to enter.

"Aisha, there's some police out here who want to speak with the owner," he said, peeking his head in the glass door.

"Send them in," she quickly replied, standing up to go greet her unwanted visitors.

Seconds later, in walked Detective Dooley, with Hill, his partner, right behind him.

"How can I help you gentlemen?" Tish asked, smiling like the perfect hostess.

Dooley stared silently at the lady like she was a perp a photo lineup.

"I'm Detective Hill, and this my partner, Detective Dooley," the young black detective said. He found himself staring at Tish, envying the tight black dress that hugged her curves. Hill almost forgot why they were there as he got lost in her brown eyes, which complemented the honey-blonde hair that hung to her shoulders.

"We're looking for the owner, Ms…?" Dooley said, taking over for his partner.

"Aisha," Tish said, finishing his question. "The owner is unavailable at the moment, but I'm the manager. Whatever you need, I'm more than happy to help you," she offered, staring at Dooley with that enticing smile still on her face.

"We're just doing a follow-up on the shooting that took place here some months back, to see if you have any further information for us," Dooley said, the excuse he'd given his partner for their trip down there.

"Yeah, that was a tragic night. I so hate that happened, especially here, but I haven't heard anything new, Detectives," she said like, sounding very sad. "Do you know if they've found Junior yet?" she asked with a little smirk on her face. "He was a dear friend of the club."

Dooley just smiled back like he'd gotten all the information he needed.

Hill chimed in, "Well, if you come up with anything—and I do mean anything—please feel free to call my number anytime." He'd finally come out of his trance and hoped she really would call him.

"Well, I might just do that," Tish said, flirting with the detective as she took the card he passed to her.

The door of the office came open behind the officers, making them turn around.

"I knew I smelled pork," No'fere said as he walked in the office, dressed in his typical all black attire, munching on some hot wings and licking the sauce off his fingers.

"And you are?" Dooley asked as the light-skinned man, who parted him and his partner like they weren't even there.

"I'm just getting here, and you're just leaving. So now

that we know each other, y'all have a night."

"I'm sure we'll meet again real soon," Dooley said, pissed off on the inside by No'fere's arrogance. *And we'll see who gets the last laugh,* Dooley thought to himself as he led his partner out the door of the office.

"Why you always gotta be so rude?" Tish said to her cousin.

He didn't answer. He just held his food out, offering her one of his messy, sticky wings.

"Move, nigga. You get on my nerves!" Tish said, laughing and admiring her cousin's arrogance at the same time. "Hurry up and finish that shit so we can go party," she ordered, sitting back down and hitting her Hennessy again before she reached down and pulled out the last once of purple kryptonite she'd been hiding from No'fere.

"See! I knew you was holding out. You gon' make me pop yo' ass, Tish."

"Well, we'll be some shot-up kryptonite-smoking muthafuckas up in here," Tish replied.

Both of them shared a laugh, but little did they know, it would be short-lived, because their next visitor would put an end to all their fun and games.

* * *

No'fere and Tish had made their way down from the office to one of the VIP sections to drink and party with some sexy ladies and associates from the club.

"Excuse me. I don't mean to bother y'all, but I got

somebody who says they want to meet y'all," the super-thick, caramel-skinned female said. She was dressed in a pink cat suit and had short hair that revealed the tattoo on her neck, two cherries with the word "Juice" inked around them.

"I'll meet anybody you want me to meet, sweetheart," Tish said. She wanted to put her pussy all over the female's face and see just how juicy she was. *"I'm gon' fuck you,"* Tish said with her lips to the female without a sound, but Juicy definitely heard her loud and clear.

"Who's your friend?" No'fere asked the female.

Before she could answer, a brown-skinned man in an all-red suit, with a matching dob hat and gator shoes, looking like a pimp from the players' ball, answered for her. "I just wanted to take some time to come over here and tell y'all how much I like the establishment. They call me Benny."

That name came crashing down on their minds like a ton of bricks. They knew of only one Benny in the city, and he'd crossed their family a long time ago. Benny didn't even need an introduction, because as he looked at No'fere and Tish, there was no denying who their parents were: No'fere looked just like Red, and Tish looked just like her real mother, the queen.

Tish wanted to kill him right there on the spot, but as she looked at No'fere, it was like she could read his mind, telling her it was not the time. "It's nice to meet you as well. I'm happy you're enjoying our club, and I hope to see you around here more often," she said with a smile.

"Drinks on us tonight. Y'all just have a good time," No'fere quickly interjected, knowing his cousin's smile could be deadly and that the situation could get out of control real quick.

"Thanks. I won't keep y'all up," Benny said, ready to leave as well.

Juicy was right behind him, and she looked back only long enough to see Tish blow a kiss at her, and that made her giggle.

Benny's mind was racing as he walked back to his section. He was kicking it in the club, knowing he was just going to stay for a little while longer, just so his real reasons for being there didn't seem too obvious. *All I had to do was tell Agent Fellows "no,"* he thought to himself, but he knew those who refused Fellows either ended up as one of the Reaper's many victims or in prison for a long time. He just shook his head as he took a long swig from the bottle of Cristal that had been sent to his table and thought back on his last meeting with Fellows.

* * *

A few days ago, the six-two, skinny, white FBI agent with dark hair had entered Benny's office. He was wearing a dark suit and glasses, and he looked like one of the Men in Black. Benny thought about mentioning that to Fellows, but he knew Fellows too well, considering he'd been selling drugs for Fellows for the last ten years. Benny just keep it to himself. *Now is not the times for jokes,* he thought, gazing at the serious look on Fellows's face.

"I know King's behind this Junior thing!" Agent Fellows said in an aggressive voice. When the news of King's appeal had hit the city, that was all people were talking about, but since some female had tried to broker a deal for Junior, whom everyone believed dead, King was yesterday's news.

"You're overreacting!" Benny said, knowing Fellow was obsessed with King and stopping him from ever walking the streets again.

"What the fuck you mean, overreacting? Were you overreacting ten years ago when you snitched your best friend's plans out to me?" Fellows quickly snapped back at Benny, pissed off that Benny would undermine him. He was even more upset, though, that even from prison, King was outsmarting them.

The words stung Benny's soul because they were true. He had sold his best friend out, a decision he'd strongly regretted over the last ten years.

"Now this is what I need you to do," Fellows said, pausing to light a Marlboro before continuing. "Go down to Club Redlight and check out a female named Aisha. They say she runs the place, and she's apparently the one who brought this Junior shit back to life. I need to know her connection to King, if any." And with that, Fellows walked out.

Benny was left standing there with a crazy look on his

face. Fellows hadn't even given him a chance to answer, let alone refuse. Benny knew that meant he had no choice but to head to Club Redlight.

* * *

Benny grabbed the bottle of Cristal again and put it back to his lips, trying to drown the shame he felt for betraying King. They had been best friends growing up, and Benny knew he had let money cloud his vision when King had told them they were going to end the dope game. Benny didn't see the big picture at the time. All he saw was that being broke was not an option, and with King out of the way, he had a chance to run things. The thing that really bothered Benny was that King knew he was going to tell, which meant King knew he was weak but loved him enough to give him the option of getting out of the game and being part of the movement. "Damn!" Benny said, thinking out loud and wishing he would've decided differently, now knowing how cutthroat Fellows was. Even though Benny had the dope game on lock and had made him and Fellows millions, he knew without a doubt that Fellows would replace him without a second thought if Benny didn't cooperate. Benny knew it was too late for apologies or to change the past, but he could change the future by not telling Fellows that the female he was asking about was King's daughter. He didn't know if King could ever forgive him, but the thought of who wouldn't forgive him made him quickly get up and tell his crew. "Let's get out of here now!" Benny knew if King's daughter was there and Red's son was there, Red couldn't be far away. Within minutes, they were out the door, all except for Juicy whom Benny told to stay back. He'd seen the way Tish was on her, and even though he was sorry for what he had done in the past, he wasn't a fool. Benny didn't know what King was going to next, but having somebody on the inside meant he could at least protect his own ass.

* * *

Fat Cats bail bond business looked like it was closed as Tish approached. A single light from a TV was all she could see, but she didn't even hesitate to enter.

At first it looked as if nobody was there ,and the TV just had static on it ,but within seconds, Fat Cat emerged from the darkness, waddling his big ass out of the back room. "Hey, sweetie! Happy you could make it. I was starting to think you weren't going to show up."

"Oh, you knew I was going to show up," Tish replied, making Fat Cat laugh.

"Well, the Italians want to meet tomorrow morning. Here's the address and time. Make sure that whoever you doing this for have my money, 'cause this a lot of risk. These Italians don't play," Fat Cat said with a straight face as he passed Tish a folded piece of paper.

Tish turned and began to walk away like she wasn't paying Fat Cat any attention, but she quickly stopped in her tracks when he began speaking again.

"How would you like to make $100,000?"

Even though it was chump change compared to the money involved with Junior, Tish quickly responded, "Money talks, and I'm listening?"

Fat Cat reached in his desk and pulled out a stack of money and threw it on the desk. "That's $50,000 now, and you'll give the other $50,000 after the fact."

"What's the job?" Tish said, walking toward the desk. She picked up the stack of money and thumbed through it like she was counting it, even though it had a $50,000 money band wrapped around it.

"I got a client that needs a package picked up. You have to go to this address," Fat Cat said, pausing as he wrote the address down on a piece of paper. "You need to go here tomorrow at 10 a.m., not a minute later. Ask for Mr. Chalmers at the front desk. Go meet him, get the package, and bring it back here."

"Sounds too easy for $100,000," she replied.

"Let's just say my client pays good, and if you do this, he might have some future work for you that'll pay even better," Fat Cat finished as he plopped down in his chair.

"All right, I'm in," Tish said, stuffing the money in her purse and walking toward the door.

"I'll be in touch," she said as she walked out the door.

Fat Cat just shook his head, knowing he had sent her into a death trap. "I hope you ready," he whispered to himself.

A voice from behind him broke his thoughts. "That's

the girl, huh?" the grimy voice of the Reaper said as he emerged from the darkness of the back room.

"Yep," Fat Cat replied, not knowing if he really wanted to answer the question or not.

The Reaper just grinned before he gave off his devilish laugh that sent a chill down Fat Cat's fat back.

* * *

It was 8:00 in the morning as the white Chevy utility van pulled up to the guarded doors of the usually abandoned warehouse that was owned by one of the two mafia families who ran different sides of the city. The two Italian guards at the garage door of the warehouse quickly approached the van to check it out. They were armed with M-16s.

The identities of the drivers and the passengers were hidden behind full ski masks. The guard on the driver side just peeked in the van and saw another masked man in the back, with an AK-47 pointed at the head of a man on his knees and a tan pillowcase on his head. The Italian guard quickly turned his head back toward the warehouse door and screamed something in Italian, and instantly the garage door that the van was sitting in front of opened up so the van could pull inside.

The upper deck of the warehouse was swarming with Italian guards, armed with machineguns. In front of them was a table with five black duffle bags on it. There were also six more machinegun-armed Italians, and in the middle of them was mafia capo Carmine "The Snake" Moreno.

The driver of the van turned the vehicle around so that the back doors were facing the awaiting Italians, and then he put it in park. The sound of the Italians' machineguns cocking filled the silence of the warehouse as the driver and the passenger of the van jumped out and began walking toward the back of the van doors.

Carmine had waited for this moment for years, and all he could do was think about revenge as the masked men opened the back of the van, exposing the other masked man, who had the gun to the head of the man on his knees with his face covered. Carmine always paid close attention to details, and he noticed that the man's hand was missing, just like he knew Junior's was. Carmine thought $5 million was a bit steep, but it was worth it to him. *I would've paid $10 million,* he thought to himself as he lit his cigar and thought back on why it had all started .

* * *

It had been a little over ten years ago, before there were two mafia families in the city, and Carmine was the only boss. Carmine had the drug game on lock, and his main moneymakers were two young black boys from the Marion Jones projects. Then, along came the Colombians, out of nowhere, trying to sell drugs without his permission and without giving him a cut. Carmine quickly set up a sit-down with the Colombian boss, El Capitan, but he was surprised to find out that El Capitan had been trying to reach out to him as well.

The meeting was put together at Carmine's deli, the front he used to handle business. Carmine had never seen El Capitan before, and not many others had either, but a boss could recognize a boss. When the door to the deli opened, four Colombians with M-16s came in, followed by a seven-foot, 300-pound, dark-haired Colombian bruiser with a long scar going across his face. Behind him was a five-seven Colombian man with a black ponytail, dressed like an army colonel. Carmine was a little nervous, even though he had six of his people around him and four more in the back. That giant looked like he could take the whole place down with no gun.

"It's nice to finally meet you!" El Capitan said in his Colombian accent, extending his hand to the hand of the approaching Carmine, who was dressed in a $10,000 black suit, as if he was going to a funeral.

"And you as well," Carmine said, shaking the man's hand.

"Now that you're here, let's get down to—"Carmine began.

He was cut off by El Capitan, who insisted on finishing his sentence. "Business." He paused for a second before continuing, "I assure you, Mr. Moreno, that what I have to say will be brief and can probably clear up this mess." Once he realized he had Carmine's full attention, he went on, "I know there's enough money for both of us to eat out here, but the only way you're going to be able to continue to make yours is to turn your operation over to me. I'll be your supplier," El Capitan said with a stern, confident face.

"Turn my operation over to you? Are you fucking serious? This guy's gotta be fucking joking," Carmine finished, turning toward his goons and laughing.

"The only other option I'm willing to consider will bring death to you, your families, and anybody who does business with you, especially the two blacks who are making you rich," El Capitan said with a calm look on his face.

Carmine hated being threatened, and he really hated when someone snooped in his business. He couldn't figure out how the man knew about his top moneymakers, King and Red. "Well, I guess this meeting is over," Carmine said. He was ready to pull his gun from his waistline and kill El Capitan right there on the spot, but he knew that warehouse was far too confined for a gun war. *It's not the time or the place,* he thought to himself as El Capitan and his goons turned around and walked out.

Letting El Capitan walk out was a decision Carmine would live to regret, because days later, El Capitan made good on his threat. Carmine had top security at his mansion, and he wanted his newborn son, his two-year-old daughter, and his wife to stay put until he discovered what El Capitan's next move was going to be. Carmine usually got up early, but he and the guys had been out late drinking, and he remained sound asleep until he heard the sound of car doors closing outside. Carmine jumped up in his boxers, alarmed because he had warned his family not to go anywhere.

He bolted downstairs and saw his newborn and the nanny, but he didn't see his wife and two-year-old. As he approached the door, he already knew his bossy wife had bullied the security into taking her somewhere, as usual. Carmine ran out of the front door and saw his white Bentley pulling off down his long driveway. Security looked at him strangely as he screamed, "Stop that car!"

The security men who were up ahead of the Bentley started flagging the car down, and Carmine ran down the driveway, ready to give his wife a good smack-down for not listening to him. The driver of the Bentley stopped, and Carmine could see his daughter in the back window, waving her little teddy bear at him as he approached like a raging bull. Then, all of a sudden, the white Bentley exploded before his eyes, knocking him off his feet from the force of the blast that killed his wife and daughter.

* * *

Carmine had lived with regret for years. He'd even stopped drinking, blaming himself for having been out the night before, getting drunk. He was sure if he hadn't slept late that morning, he could have stopped that tragedy from happening. He even had regret for not warning King and Red of the threat toward them and their families. It had been a long wait for revenge, but Carmine hoped it would all be over now.

The voice of one of the masked men broke his train of

thought. "Are we going to do this today or tomorrow?" the masked man on the driver side said.

"Send me the boy!" Carmine demanded.

"Money first!" the masked man yelled back. Carmine wasn't in the mood to play games, and he could see that they had the boy, so he quickly yelled something in Italian to his goons, sending them into action. Within seconds, the five bags, each containing a million dollars, were on the ground in front of the masked men in front of the van. The passenger of the van wasted no time unzipping bag by bag, making sure the money was there.

"Okay, okay. Do you want to count it all or what? Let's get this shit over with. I got shit to do!" Carmine yelled out as his four goons waited for the masked men to give them Junior.

The masked passenger looked up at the driver and gave him a nod, letting him know the money was official.

The masked driver began speaking again. "The price tag just went up to $20 million, we will be taking this as a deposit," he said, causing the Italians around the warehouse to take aim.

"Yeah, $20 million, huh?" Carmine said. He paused for a moment and smiled at his goons, who had reacted without him saying anything; that made him proud. "The $5 million was a gesture of my good faith, but I see you are taking my kindness for a weakness. I could just kill you and keep my money," Carmine said, hungry to see them die for trying to cross him.

"How did I know you were going to say that?" the masked driver said, looking at his masked passenger, who looked back at him, shaking his head and smiling.

Carmine's goons had their fingers on the trigger, ready to squeeze it the second Carmine gave the order to kill.

Carmine was furious at the actions of the masked men and was ready to tell his goons to kill them all, but the masked man in the back of the van, with the gun to the head of the $5 million man, snatched the pillowcase off his head. The abrupt movement almost sent the warehouse up in gunfire, but everybody froze, including Carmine, as he looked in the eyes off his son, little Carmine, with duct tape covering his lips and a rifle to the back of his head.

* * *

It was 10 a.m. when Tish walked in front of the sky-scraper with mirrored windows. The address was 377, just like on the paper she had in her hand, the one she'd gotten from Fat Cat the night before. She wasn't surprised that the time of the exchange for Junior and the time for her to be there were the same. She wished she could've been there ,but she knew she had to focus, especially since she noticed that even though the streets were busy outside the building, nobody was going in or out of the building.

As Tish walked inside the building in her cream business outfit with matching Louis Vuitton purse and glasses, looking like she owned the place, she glanced at the old white receptionist. The lady's hair was completely white, and in her bright red outfit, she looked like Mrs. Clause. She was busy answering the phones, which seemed to be ringing off the hook.

"Hold please," she said to someone on her headset as Tish approached. "How may I help you?" she asked, talking to Tish.

"I'm looking for Mr. Chalmers's office."

"He's on the thirtieth floor," the receptionist quickly shot out.

"Thank you," Tish said. She walked to the elevator, just past reception to the right. She pushed the up button and watched as the elevator descended from the fortieth floor, the penthouse. As the elevator started coming down, Tish quickly turned around to ask the receptionist what the name of Mr. Chalmers's company was, but Mrs. Clause was no longer at her desk. It was silent except for the clicking of her six-inch heels as she went to the front door of the building and tried to open it. As Tish put her hands on the door handle of the building, she could see that from the inside of the door the view to the outside was blurry, to the point where she could barely make out the people who were walking down the street. She pushed on the door, but it didn't budge. She began to beat on it, trying to get someone's attention, but it seemed like nobody could hear her; everyone just continued walking by, no matter how hard she banged on the door.

Suddenly, she heard a noise from behind her that let her know what she was supposed to do next. The lobby lights went out, and metal shutters rolled down over the windows, leaving her in total darkness other than the bright light from the elevator door that had opened up down the hall. Tish stood there for a few seconds, admiring the creativity of whoever was playing the game with her, and then she walked toward the elevator, stepped inside, and pushed the right button to close the doors and send the elevator ascending to the thirtieth floor.

Tish's mood was cooler than the other side of the pillow as she stood there popping her bubble gum through her lip gloss, as if she didn't care that she'd just been locked in a building by herself. She nonchalantly hummed to the elevator music as the elevator rose floor by floor. Tish was loving the "I Will Always Love You" tune by Whitney Houston that played softly through the speakers of the elevator, and she almost found herself singing the words, but the ringing of a phone got her attention, making her look down toward a little door on the wall that said, "Use in case of emergencies." When she opened the door, something fell on the floor. It looked like an earpiece of some sort, so she picked it up to examine it before she picked up the ringing red phone. "How may I help you?" Tish asked, holding the phone receiver next to her ear.

"I'm happy you could join me today. Thank you for accepting the challenge," the grimy voice said through the other end of the phone.

"What challenge?" Tish quickly snapped back. "I don't know shit about no challenges. I'm here to meet someone."

"Oh, I assure you you're going to meet a lot of people today," the man said, followed by a small, sinister laugh before he started talking again.

"Walking in the front door was your acceptance of more than just a challenge. It's also an opportunity to come work for me."

"And who are you that I would want to work for you?" Tish quickly snapped.

"They call me the Reaper."

"Well, Mr. Reaper, what if I don't want to work for you?"

"Well, Ms Aisha," the Reaper began, calling her by the name Fat Cat had told him, "then this is where you will die! If you want to live, I advise that you put that earpiece in your ear and follow my instructions very carefully."

Tish quickly put the earpiece in her ear so she could hear the Reaper as she walked, but when the elevator reached its floor, the doors didn't open.

"Good. Now that we have an understanding, there is only one rule in this challenge. That is that you must stay alive," the Reaper said.

"Well, that probably won't be hard," Tish replied as she reached in her big Chanel purse that looked more like a book bag. She pulled out a pair of black Air Max shoes and dropped them to the floor. Then she reached into her bag and retrieved a black SIG-Sauer P220 Colt .45 automatic handgun and cocked it .

"I like," the Reaper said, pausing. "I see you've come prepared."

"Yeah. There's no telling when a stranger is going to lock you in an elevator, talking about living is the only rule," Tish said, mocking the Reaper.

He wasn't usually known for his sense of humor, but he took amusement in the girl's sass, especially considering her current situation. He actually wanted her to make it through, because he needed a new protégé, especially considering the female he knew as Aisha had had something to do with the deaths of his two white female protégés that were found sliced up in the penthouse where their target, Junior, had disappeared from eight months back. *Now it's time to play,* he thought to himself.

"Let's do this shit. I got a date tonight," Tish said as she stood there in her black Air Max, gripping her gun with both hands, ready to kill.

"Yes. Let the games began," he said as he allowed the doors of the elevator to open up.

"About damn time!" Tish whispered to herself, thinking out loud.

* * *

As the masked man in the back of the van pressed the barrel of his AK-47 against the head of little Carmine, big Carmine just hoped none of his goons had an itchy trigger finger. "Hold your fire!" he yelled. He wasn't prepared to lose his only son, and even though he hated having to back down, he knew it was a no-win situation. All he could do was comply with their demands. "Okay, okay! Whatever! Just don't hurt my son!" he yelled to the kidnappers.

"Good. We will be in touch…and, oh yea, El Capitan sends his regards," the masked driver said as the passenger loaded the bags of money into the van and closed the door, with little Carmine inside. "When I call this phone, you answer." He threw one of Carmine's goons a cell phone, and then he and the passenger got back in the van.

Carmine knew there was a chance he might never see his son alive again, but if there was a way to save his life, he was willing to try. "Let them go!" Carmine yelled, and within seconds, the garage door to the warehouse was open, and the van pulled out, leaving the stunned Italians behind.

Little Carmine tried to scream through the duct tape, but his cries were cut short by the masked man bringing the butt of the AK down on the back of his head, knocking him unconscious.

"Damn, Fere. Don't kill the boy!" Red said as he took his ski mask off and drove.

"My bad, Pops!" No'fere replied, even though he'd hit little Carmine that hard on purpose.

"Sucka!" Sam said from the passenger seat, messing with No'fere as usual.

"I'm starting to think that's the only word you know," No'fere said back to Sam; he made it a habit to always call No'fere a sucka, like it was his nickname.

"I don't need to know no more muthafucking words. My bitch talk for me," Sam said, pulling out a Smith and Wesson 500. He took pride in bragging about the weapon, saying it was the world's largest handgun and that it wouldn't be out on the market for years to come.

The men just laughed, but on the inside none of them were laughing. They knew Tish was on her own, and there was nothing they could do about it but sit and wait and hope she didn't get killed.

That thought was weighing very heavily on Red's soul. The original plan had been to use No'fere instead of Tish to get the attention of the Reaper, but Tish had insisted, and Red really need No'fere for another mission. *Plus, it's so hard to say "no" to her,* Red thought to himself, shaking his head as he drove. Red always kept people on a need-to-know basis, and nobody knew that part of the plan to get King out was to kidnap Junior. They knew that would trigger the Reaper to go scouting for talent to join his infamous hit squad, and then they could finally have somebody on the inside, there when the predictable Agent Fellows decided to call his favorite hit man, the Reaper, to take the King out. Red cracked a grin. He knew his niece was nothing to be played with. If she did what she was supposed to, King could be free after all those years. The need for Junior and Carmine was over, as far as their plan was concerned, but Red could see nothing but revenge. *Yeah, this personal, muthafuckas,* he thought to himself as Sam and No'fere continued to argue back and forth, not paying him any attention. "Come home, baby girl," he whispered under his breath, hoping he wouldn't live to regret his decision to knowingly let his niece Tish—a young woman who was more like his daughter—walk into a death trap.

* * *

As the doors of the elevator came open, Tish stood there gripping her .45 tightly. She looked across the fancy business office, but she saw no movement among the cubicles and glass-enclosed rooms. "I advise you to step outside the elevator immediately. In twenty seconds, the doors will close, and the elevator will, in essence, become a gas chamber—your tomb if you do not comply."

Tish squatted low and began to creep out of the elevator, but the machinegun fire from the blind spots on the left and the right sides stopped her in her tracks. She could hear bullets whizzing by, just inches from her face, and landing close to her. She popped back in the elevator, giggling. "Cute!" Tish said.

"Ten seconds," the Reaper replied, laughing.

His two newly trained hit men waited outside the elevator door, M-16s at the ready, for their target to come back out. The two assassins waited patiently, knowing she only had a few seconds left. When the doors of the elevator began to close, the gunmen started to relax, assuming she was scared.

In the next second, right when the doors reached the

point when it looked like nobody could fit through, Tish came diving out, across the hallway.

The assassins barely saw her, but they squeezed their triggers again, shooting recklessly at a target that was no longer there. It was as if their nervous fingers were glued to the trigger, and they emptied their weapons, almost killing each other in the process. The assassin on the left quickly grabbed a clip out of his pocket, but he was too late; a .45 bullet ripped into his hand, preventing him from grabbing the clip, and another hit him high in his chest, almost simultaneously dropping him dead to the floor. The other assassin froze when he saw Tish spin back around his direction and squeeze the trigger of her gun again. She had a smile on her face as she sent the bullet spiraling down the hallway and right into the middle of his forehead.

"That was nice!" the Reaper said in her earpiece, admiring her precision.

"You ain't seen nothing yet. I'm just getting warmed up, baby," she replied. When she heard the shuffling of feet from behind her, Tish turned back around, ready to shoot again, but nobody was there. She looked down the six rows of cubicles before the offices at the back where anybody could be hiding.

"There's a bag in the corner office. Go get it," the Reaper said.

How did I know he was going to say that? Tish thought to herself, right before another assassin jumped out of the third cubicle on the right side.

The wannabe killer began firing rapid rounds with his machinegun, shooting scared, especially after he'd heard the first line of defense get killed. His nerves would be his mistake.

Tish never even moved; she didn't need to since the wild bullets from the machinegun didn't even come close to hitting her.

The assassin, on the other hand, wasn't as lucky as she squeezed off three bullets: One hit him in his thigh, taking him down to his knees; another slammed into his chest, forcing him to drop the gun he was still shooting; and the final shot hit him right above his left eye, leaving him lifeless.

Tish moved forward, staying low and creeping aisle by aisle, watching for anybody that might pop out at her. To her surprise, no one did. "Wow! You call that a challenge? Too easy," Tish mocked with laughter, knowing something wasn't right.

"Corner office. Hurry," he replied.

Tish moved toward the office swiftly but cautiously. She could see through the glass walls of the office; it didn't seem anyone was inside—just a desk with a chair behind it and black bag on it. She made her way in the office, still being precautious.

"I thought I'd help you out a little bit. I'm sure you'll need the items in the bag," the Reaper said.

Tish went to the bag and began to unzip it, but she was interrupted by a warning from the Reaper.

"Uh-oh! I think you got company," he said in her ear, laughing.

Tish looked up to see the front glass wall of the office come smashing in from machinegun fire. She grabbed the bag and hit the floor, then ducked behind the desk. Bullets ripped through the office, shattering the windows behind her. Splintered fragments of the desk flew everywhere, like shrapnel. The heavy machinegun fire went on for at least a minute, leaving the office bullet riddled and full of holes.

"You okay?" the Reaper taunted in her earpiece, laughing again.

"They done fucked my hair up," Tish replied, right before she heard another sound.

Tink...tink...tink...

She knew exactly what that sound was, and her suspicion was confirmed when she saw the teargas grenade go rolling by. In an instant, it exploded, releasing the stinging gas into the room.

Twenty rogue U.S. marshals had taken them upon themselves to get back at whoever had been responsible for the deaths of their officers six month earlier. The captain had been quite happy to receive the tip from the Reaper that morning that the person they were looking for would be in that office building. "Unit 1, go get her!" the captain said, motioning for the five-man squad to make their approach.

The squad was dressed in black S.W.A.T. team gear, and within seconds, they disappeared into the thick teargas smoke. The sound of gunfire erupted in the office, but the captain couldn't give the command to shoot in blindly, with his men inside. As the teargas began to clear, the gunfire stopped, leaving everything in an eerie, dead silence. When the smoked cleared, the captain's heart dropped; he could see two of his men lying dead across the top of the desk and the other three stretched out on the floor. One of the officers was still moving, trying to crawl across the floor. The captain's first instinct was to go rescue his wounded man, but that would prove to be a fatal mistake.

As soon as he got ready to give the words, Tish jumped up from behind the desk. She was no longer in her business clothes. Her hair that had been hanging loose before was now tied back in a ponytail. Her skirt had been replaced with little black shorts, a perfect complement for the black sports bra and something that looked like a small backpack. "So, y'all wanna throw shit ,huh?" she said from under the piece of fabric on her mouth. She'd torn it off her blouse and wisely wet it with the bottle of water she'd found in the bag the Reaper had left for her so she could withstand the teargas.

The captain's eyes grew wide as saucers as he saw the four smoke grenades she held, two in each hand.

Tish wasted no time throwing the grenades in their direction. The grenades rolled in between the U.S. marshals, who tried to retreat, to no avail. It was too late, because the thick black smoke covered them like a black blanket, making it impossible to see.

"Stay tight!" the captain said, right before a .45 bullet ripped into the side of his face.

The men's training had taught them not to panic, but that did them no good. They began to shoot sporadically and frantically in the direction of where they'd seen the girl, hoping not to shoot one another in the process.

Unfortunately for them, Tish was now behind them, and she quickly made them aware of their mistake, as she squeezed the trigger of the M4 machinegun she'd taken off one of the dead marshals in the office. She aimed low, chopping six of the men down easily; she didn't kill them, but she managed to knock their legs out from under them.

"Sounds like you out of bullets," the Reaper teased in her earpiece, anxious to see what she was going to do next as he watched from across the street with his thermal goggles.

"They bad!" she replied with a devilish giggle.

The six men she'd chopped down rolled around on the floor, writhing in pain from the multiple gunshots to their lower limbs, screaming like little girls. The three remaining rogue marshals were finally able to see through the smoke; they had strategically stood back to back, ready to shoot at the sign of any movement. One of the marshals saw something, but it was too late to squeeze the trigger, as a he felt his tactical knife being snatched from its holster on his leg and slammed into the side of his neck. Before the marshal to the left could react, Tish had pulled the knife out of his partner's neck and spun around backward to stab him right in the middle of his throat. Another marshal turned to get a shot off, but all he did was hit his own partner in the back as he fell to the floor from the knife wound in his throat. Next, he felt the knife stab him deep in his thigh. The pain sent him down to one knee, and he dropped his gun as he fell. Next thing he knew, he was face to face with Tish. She snatched the knife out of the man's legs tearing his flesh open, and stuck it right up through the bottom of his chin, trying to put it in his brain. The smoke in the room had almost completely disappeared as she walked by the six men on the floor, struggling to live.

Tish promptly pulled her .45 from her back and executed the six, putting bullets in their heads one by one, showing not the slightest bid of hesitation, mercy, or remorse. "*Now* I'm out of bullets," she said as she stood there with the gun cocked back, ready for her to feed it another clip.

"In that case, I think you should run," the Reaper responded.

She looked up, out of the skylight window, only to see a menacing black helicopter hovering above. In the copter were three more marshals. The pilot slid the side door of the helicopter door open. Another marshal sat behind the same type of helicopter gun that had been used to kill the fallen marshals back at the Waltz Hotel. The gunner could see the floor of the office building, littered with the bodies of dead marshals, and he quickly turned his attention toward Tish, who seemed to make direct eye contact with him right before he pulled the trigger of the gun.

Tish saw the six barrels of the gun began to rotate around in a circle, and she knew she had to move fast, even though the weapon would begin to fire slowly. Just as the first bullet came out of the gun, she made her move, dashing back to the corner office. She was as swift as a cheetah in the jungle, and the gunfire was right on her heels every step of the way, ripping round after round through the shattered and smoky office building.

The sounds of police and S.W.A.T. teams echoed up from the streets below, but the rogue marshals in the helicopter continued their demolition, not willing to leave without their revenge. The gunner couldn't see his target from where he was, so he ordered the pilot to circle around the building. The side window of the corner office was still intact, and the blinds were still closed, making it impossible for the gunner to shoot through, since he didn't know if any of his men were still alive and trapped inside. The windows were already blown out on the back side of the building, so he rounded the helicopter there, hoping to find a view straight through the office.

"Keep going!" the gunner yelled over the loud helicopter propellers as the pilot pulled the gunner around. The gunner was ready to get the gun rotating. He was not happy that the girl had eluded him before, but he halted the gun in half-rotation and let his finger off the trigger when he saw his target standing there, using a wounded marshal like a human shield.

Her .45, which she'd reloaded with her last clipped,

was pressed aggressively against his head. The wounded officer could barely stand on his feet with her arm around his neck, bending him backward. He had a bullet hole in each legs. The standoff was serious, but it got even more serious as the police and S.W.A.T. team filled the office where the dead marshals and the Reapers hit man were.

"Put the gun down!" one of the S.W.A.T. members yelled to Tish.

She turned quickly, jerking her hostage around. "Fuck you! I WILL kill him!" she yelled back from under her blouse mask she had made to hide her identity.

The S.W.A.T. team wasn't about to play with her and quickly started moving closer and closer as the helicopter hovered behind her, waiting for a clear shot.

"Hmm. Looks like you're in a bit of a bind," the Reaper said in her earpiece.

"Naw. I got them right where I want 'em," she replied, watching the S.W.A.T. team and police move closer and closer, ignoring her threat to kill her hostage. "I see you muthafuckas hard-headed," Tish said as the S.W.A.T. team and police took their positions around the office.

"This the last time we're going to tell you to put the gun down!" one of the S.WA.T. members yelled.

Tish just giggled, knowing they had fallen right in her trap. "You want him? Well, here he come!" she said under her breath. She released her left arm from around his neck and grabbed the pins out of the three flash grenades that were on his vest, and then she kicked him forward toward them. The explosion of the grenades flashed the whole room like a strobe light, leaving the S.W.A.T. team disoriented. In one fluid movement, before the gunner could start the gun up again, she turned around and pulled the trigger of her .45 two times. The first bullet hit the pilot in the side of the head, and the second hit the gunner in his face, knocking him off the gun. Tish didn't hesitate to jump right into the next step in her plan. She turned toward the side window before the S.W.A.T. team could recover from the flash bang and pushed the desk that was in the room right through the side window that had the blinds still closed. She quickly jumped on top of it just as the helicopter crashed into the floor beneath them exploding. The force from the blast was like a kick in the back, and it sent her flying toward the building across the street in a hurry. She almost lost consciousness, but her adrenalin wouldn't allow it.

The Reaper had left another gift for her in the bag, and it proved to be helpful in this moment; she reached around her back with her free hand and pulled the ripcord. The black parachute deployed, slowing her down, but she was approaching the tenth floor of the adjacent building far too quickly, destined to make a painful crash landing. Instinctively, Tish took aim at the windows of the building and began shooting. Then, she braced herself for impact, not wanting to die like a bug on the windshield. The .45 bullets shattered the glass just as she hit the window, softening her impact, but it was a punishing landing, and it knocked the air out of her, leaving her disoriented as she lay there in a pile of broken glass.

"Let me know if you wanna quit," the Reaper tempted in her earpiece.

Tish didn't respond right away. Her first thought was to gather her parachute and pull it in, knowing if she didn't, the wind could catch it and drag her right back out the window.

"You still there.?" The Reaper asked, hearing her breathing heavily.

"I ain't never left!" she replied.

"Good. Meet me on the street on the back side of the building. I'm coming to get you."

Tish immediately took off running toward the far side of the building, with her parachute balled up under her arm. The building had been evacuated, so she easily ran full speed across the office floor till she was ten feet from the windows of the far side of the building. She smiled as she aimed her .45 again and shot at the window in front of her, knocking it out. Tish never stopped moving; every stride felt like she was moving in slow motion. She jumped right out the window, letting go of the balled up parachute that popped back open like it had never been used before. She quickly descended ten floors till the concrete of the street was beneath the soles of her Air Max shoes. She pulled her chute off as she looked down at the empty street.

As soon as she got it off, two police cars came flying around the corner, coming her direction. When they got within twenty feet of her, her attention was drawn to the racing of an engine behind her, causing her to turn around.

"Get down !" the Reaper said in her earpiece.

Tish hit the ground immediately as she watched a black van speeding her direction. She was trapped on the ground between the van and the four police officers who'd exited their cars; the police had their guns drawn, ready to make an arrest. The black van looked like it wasn't going to stop ,but Tish didn't budge. Then, all of a sudden, the brakes of the van squealed and screeched to a halt, and the driver spun the whole van around. The back doors flew open, aimed directly at the police. The officers froze at the sight, and cost them dearly. The bark of the AR-15 was just as deadly as its bite, as the Reaper squeezed the trigger, sending a shower of bullets at the police cars. The fire of the AR-15 showed no prejudice, ripping into the police cars and two of the four officers that were trying to hide behind them.

"Let's go!" the Reaper yelled.

Tish jumped to her feet instantly and dove in the back of the van just as it got ready to pull off. The van peeled off toward the corner it had come from and turned left just as another police car was getting ready to turn on to the street, barely missing them. The Reaper smiled as he took aim at the police car in pursuit; the driver was desperately trying to follow the van while he radioed in for backup, but he never had a chance to call for help before the AR-

15 bullets pounded down into the front of his car and into him, sending him swerving into a light pole to meet his death.

"Welcome to the family!" the Reaper said, looking at Tish.

She stood up and finally took off her makeshift mask. "Thank you," she replied, smiling and knowing on the inside that she was one step closer to being with her real family.

The Reaper had a squad of killers in his arsenal, but he had never met any like her. He knew with some work, she could either be his number one pupil or his number one threat, and he was willing to find out which. He sure wasn't going to tell Agent Fellows about her, considering that Fellows had sent him down to Fat Cat's bail bonds to check her out. And with that thought, they disappeared into traffic

* * *

With the news of everything that had gone down that day, Fat Cat was pissed off. He was all about money, after all, and he hadn't received his cut for brokering the Junior deal with the Italians. "Bitch, I said hurry the fuck up and go get my food!" the fat man yelled to one of his hoes as she hurried out the door; Fat Cat could be dangerous when he was hungry and she didn't want any trouble. A couple seconds after the girl left, the bells on the top of the door jingled again. Fat Cat didn't even bother looking before he snapped, "Bitch, what you forget? Your brain?"

With a scowl on his face, he turned toward the door, only to see a light-skinned man standing there, dressed in black from head to toe, with dreadlocks hanging down his face. Fat Cat quickly sat up in his chair and grabbed the handle of the sawed off shotgun he kept under his desk, beneath the rolls of his massive belly. "How can I help you?" he said, changing his tone and caressing the trigger of the shotgun.

"I heard you the one to talk to if I got a problem," the man with the dreadlocks said, walking closer to the desk and reaching in his coat.

"Depends on what the problem is," Fat Cat said, nervous and ready to shoot.

"Let's say I got a $50,000 problem!" the man said. He slowly pulled his hand out of his coat and threw a stack of money on the desk with a $50,000 money band wrapped around it.

"Then I'd say you in the right place," Fat Cat replied, releasing his grip on the gun and picking up the money.

"I need somebody to disappear," the man said. He reached back into his coat and pulled out a photo, then threw it on the man's desk.

Fat Cat thumbed through the money like it was the only thing in the room and almost didn't see the picture hit the desk. He slowly looked over at the photo, and his eyes grew big; he knew the man in the picture very well. Fat Cat couldn't believe he was looking at a picture of himself, and it almost froze him up. When his visitor pulled out a black .40-caliber handgun from the back of his waistband, Fat Cat reached for the shotgun under the desk. The fat man was fast for his size, and he pulled the shotgun from its holster in one smooth motion. Unfortunately for him, his bulging belly got in his way and made his thick finger slip against the trigger, causing him to take a blast from his own shotgun that almost ripped his own left leg off. Fat Cat's screams were loud, but the laughter from the light-skinned, dreadlock man were almost just as loud.

"Not today, fat boy," the man said, pausing so he could stop laughing. "My cousin said you can keep the money, you fat fuck!" he said before he shot Fat Cat four time in his chest and one more in his forehead.

Fat Cat slumped back in his chair, a bloody, lifeless blob with a pile of money in front of him.

The killer was getting ready to walk away, but he stopped abruptly and turned around. "Fuck Tish talking about? I'm not leaving no $50,000 dollars behind for some dead, fat fuck," No'fere said, wiping the dreadlocks out of his face so he could see as he grabbed the blood-splattered money and turned back around to walk out the same door he'd come through, thinking about what he was going to spend the money on. Ten minutes later only to see the pimp that she hated so much dead. The girl didnt shed a tear as she turned around with the food she was sent to retrieve and turned back around like she never been there.

CHAPTER FIVE

All or Nothing

For the last four months, the streets had been full of bloodshed and bullet holes, thanks to the Colombians and Italians. It was just like back in the old days, when the Colombians had first tried to take over, except this time, the battle was not for dope and territory. Now, it was for vengeance; both sides thought the other were holding their sons hostage. The war in the streets made it hard for either side to make money, and both sides had suffered massive casualties, with revenge as there fuel.

Eventually, Bull, the mob boss of the city, said to Carmine, "Look, this beef has to stop. People back home are getting a little nervous, thinking you can't handle your little problem."

Carmine knew what that meant: Stop the war or stop breathing. It was an easy decision for Carmine, even though he felt like he hadn't properly avenged his son. Carmine felt defeated, but when he got the phone call from little Carmine assuring him that he was all right and that the kidnappers wanted him to bring $20 million for his return, he felt like he just might win after all. Carmine wasted no time getting the money together. He didn't care how much it would cost him; as long as his son still had breath in his body, he was willing to pay.

Two days later, Carmine found himself back in his warehouse, the same place where he'd gotten ripped off months ago. Only this time, he had an unlikely guest. Carmine was almost shocked when El Capitan, followed by a van with $20 million in it, pulled into the warehouse. Carmine stood there in his expensive black suit, looking like he had been drinking heavily and hadn't slept in years. His rival, El Capitan, looked as though he hadn't changed a bit since the first time they'd met. He still wore his Cornel uniform with pride; the only difference was that his black beard, which was now speckled with a great abundance of gray.

The two bosses were both confused by each other's presence, considering they'd both thought each other responsible. Now, they knew they were both targets, and they wasted no time in putting their minds together to try to find out who would have it out for both of them.

That question was quickly answered when the garage door burst open and a white van pulled in, followed by an armored truck, all black.

"Let's just give them their money and get this over with!" Carmine said, not feeling the least bit safe. The kidnappers had ordered the two bosses to only bring two workers each to load and unload the money and one bodyguard a piece for safety, and both he and El Capitan has complied. In this moment, he wished he hadn't and had brought more backup.

"I agree," El Capitan responded, watching the van and armored truck turn around so the back of the vehicles were facing them.

The two bosses' bodyguards pulled their guns out, ready for whatever might happen. *Damn! El Capitan's giant of a bodyguard doesn't even look like he needs a gun,* Carmine thought to himself, looking at his biggest bruiser, who didn't even compare in size.

The driver of the armored truck jumped out, a brown-skinned man with pork chop sideburns and an afro. His clothing was as black as the truck he'd jumped out of. Neither boss recognized him, but they stared at his every move as he walked toward the back of the white van and opened the door. Both bosses' hearts skipped a beat when they saw Junior and little Carmine inside the van, on their knees. Each hostage was missing a hand, and a light-skinned man dressed in black was pointing an AK-47 at them. Other than their missing hands, the bosses' sons looked to be in good shape.

Suddenly, the bosses' attention as drawn toward the driver door of the white van. As it came open, a face emerged—a face neither of them would ever forget.

"Red!" Carmine said, thinking out loud and causing El Capitan to try to remember where he'd heard the name before.

Red stepped out of the van. He, too, was dressed in

black, and his hair was in six cornrolls, going toward the back of his head. He smiled his golden grin as his eyes made instant contact with El Capitan.

The name Red still bounced around in El Capitan's brain, even after he saw the man step out of the van, but it was that grin and that frigid stare that triggered in his mind who Red was. At that moment, he knew exactly why all of it was happening.

Red continued to look at the man. Few knew what El Capitan looked like, but Red knew he had seen the man before. Then it hit him like a ton of bricks: That man had been in the backseat of the black Benz that rode by his house years earlier, right before his wife and daughter were slaughtered in front of him. *Yeah, muthafucka, I knew I'd see you again,* Red thought to himself, actually surprised that the famous El Capitan was the one he'd been looking for, the one he'd been hoping for all those years to personally pay back. "It don't get no better than this!" Red said, walking toward the two bosses and their bodyguards, with Sam right behind him and No'fere keeping the AK aimed at the hostages.

As the two black men approached, El Capitan tapped his monster of a bodyguard, Grande (which, of course, means "big" in Spanish) and whispered in his ear. The giant, who had to bend down to his boss's level, listened as El Capitan filled him in on who Red was. Grande had been driving the night Red's family was killed. The beast instantly growled and gritted his teeth as he rose back up, showing his height and looking at Red.

Red lightly nodded his head, like he was telling the giant, *"Yeah, mothafucka, it's me!"*

"Red, I heard you were dead," Carmine said as Red and Sam stood before them.

"I guess you heard wrong!" Red replied, almost laughing. Carmine had been the one to start the rumor that he was dead, considering Carmine didn't warn Red and King about the danger his family was in. "Let's get this shit over with," Red said, glaring at El Capitan, who had a devilish grin on his face.

"Well, get on with it then," El Capitan said.

The two bosses quickly told their workers to unload the money from their vans and load it in the armored truck. Sam oversaw the transfer of the money, and every so often, he randomly checked some of the black bags to make sure the cash was there; $40 million was to be loaded into the armored truck, and there was no way he could count every dollar right then. Within twenty minutes, the four workers had loaded the armored truck with $40 million, duffle bag by duffle bag. Once they were done, they gave the okay to their bosses.

Red was just staring at them, especially Grande, who was mugging Red right back.

"So are you here to rip us off or what?" Carmine asked, impatient to get his son back and get out of there.

Red just laughed before he whistled to No'fere, who nudged the two hostages with the tip of the AK to let them know they were free to go. "Nice doing business with you gentlemen," Red said, getting ready to turn around and walk away.

Junior and little Carmine made their way out of the van and across the warehouse, walking like both of them had stomachaches. They were anxious to be back with their families.

Red had only gotten two steps when the words of El Capitan stopped him in his tracks.

"Now, surely you didn't think I was going to let you walk away with my money, did you?" he said, dialing a number on his phone and hanging up before anyone answered. Instantly, the door of the warehouse came open behind the van and the armored truck. El Capitan had never had any intention of letting anyone walk away with $20 million of his money, and he just smiled as he looked at his four soldiers that had took position at the garage door of the warehouse, machineguns in hand. His two workers had also pulled their weapons out, and they had one aimed at Sam and the other aimed at Red. It was a well-orchestrated plan. Not only did El Capitan get his son back, but he was also going to leave with an extra $20 million and his enemies at his disposal.

"Hold the fuck up!" Carmine said, watching his two workers hit the ground, trying not to get shot.

No'fere pointed the AK in the direction of little Carmine and Junior, who had stopped in their tracks and put their remaining hands up in the air.

"Looks like we have a bit of a standoff, my friends!" El Capitan said in a smooth voice and casting a glance to his bodyguard.

Grande had snatched Carmine's much smaller bodyguard up by his neck with two hands and lifted him off the floor, leaving his feet dangling as the man grasped for life.

"What standoff!?" Red replied, not even turning around.

His words seemed to come with a toe tag for two of El Capitan's four soldiers who were guarding the exit. The Colombian soldier on the end never even heard a sound as Tish pulled the trigger of the .50-caliber sniper rifle from an abandoned warehouse window about 200 yards away, using her new skill the Reaper had taught her over the last few months. The bullet ripped through the man's back, leaving a gaping hole in his stomach. The other three men didn't know what was happening, but the soldier on the other end quickly found out when another .50-caliber round took his entire head off, busting his skull open like a watermelon. The other two soldiers quickly surrendered, throwing their guns on the floor and getting face down as fast as they could, praying for mercy.

El Capitan's soldiers were frozen, not knowing if the sniper would shoot them next, but it wasn't the sniper fire they should've been worried about. Sam cracked a small grin, as if he could smell the fear of the Colombian worker who was pointing the 9mm at him. As soon as the man blinked, Sam's right hand reached across his chest and under his black jacket and pulled out the massive nickel-plated Smith and Wesson 500 handgun and pulled the trigger. The deafening sound of the gun echoed through the warehouse like a bomb going off, and the bullet hit the Colombian worker right in the middle of his chest, sending him flying about three feet and rendering his nine useless. The shot left him with a hole the size of a hockey puck in his back. Sam's moves were fluid, like lightning, as he reached with his left hand across his body, into the right side of his coat, and pulled out a matching nickel-plated Smith and Wesson 500 and pulled the trigger. When the worker who had his gun on Red heard his partner go down, his heart skipped a beat, but the sound of the second shot paralyzed him with fear right before the bullet almost knocked his back into his chest, leaving him paralyzed with death.

"I think you should put him down and save your strength," Red said, turning around to look at Carmine's bodyguard, on the verge of being unconscious.

But it was as if Grande was in a trance. The giant squeezed even more tightly on the man's windpipes, almost crushing them.

"Grande!" El Capitan screamed!

The giant seemed to instantly snap out of it and threw the almost unconscious man to the floor at the feet of Carmine, who didn't know what to do next or what was going to happen next.

"I should kill all of you for pulling a move like that!"

Red said before he was cut off by Carmine.

"Red, I had nothing to do with it!" Carmine said, trying to plead his case.

"Shut up, bitch!" Red quickly snapped back before continuing with what he was saying.

"Like I was saying, I should kill you muthafuckas for pulling some shit like that, but I'm gon' do something better than that. I'm going to give y'all the chance to get your money back...and keep your kids," Red said, getting the full attention of the two bosses .

"I'm listening !" El Capitan said.

"It's simple. All he gotta do is take it take it back from me," Red said, pointing at Grande right before he cracked his knuckles, like he was ready to fight.

El Capitan smiled and looked at his giant, who looked back at him. "Go get our money back!" El Capitan said to his beast, whom he had all confidence in. As far as he was concerned, it was like a fight in Vegas, with 100/1 odds in his favor. He gave Red the nod, indicating that they would happily accept the challenge.

Carmine couldn't believe what was going on, but he was actually curious to see the two bruisers collide, and so were No'fere and Sam. No'fere had taken a seat on the edge of the van, with his AK still aiming at Junior and little Carmine; both boys looked like they were about to fall over from holding their hands up for so long. Sam just stood there smiling, with his two hand canons at his side, looking at Red.

As red pulled his black gloves out of his back pocket, Grande stepped forward, ready for the challenge. Red took off his jacket, displaying his black wife-beater that hugged his NFL linebacker physique, barely covering up the "My brother's keeper" tattoo that ran around the top of his chest. Grande had a good six inches and 100 pounds on Red as the two squared off. Red put his dukes up, barely hiding his golden smile, but Grande just laughed at the man's courage right before he charged Red like a raging bull. He had his long, gargantuan arms out, ready to choke Red and punish him severely for challenging him. Grande was six steps away, but his long legs meant it would only be three strides for him.

Red looked like he was waiting calmly, but all of a sudden, he put his shoulder down. He went from zero to sixty in seconds, heading back toward Grande. Red's move was perfectly timed, and he went right under the man's reach and rammed his right shoulder into the man's midsection like a bulldozer. Like a clothesline move in wrestling, the blow swept the giant off his feet and onto his back. The bigger they are, the harder they fall, and Grande hit the ground hard, but his pride was more hurt than anything. "You wanna wrestle, or we gon' fight?" Red asked, looking down at Grande.

The big man was trying to catch his breath. He wasn't back to 100 percent, but his anger and embarrassment fueled him quickly back to his feet. Just as Red put his guard up, Grande swung a vicious right, but Red ducked it with ease. Grande followed with a left that he hung out there way too long, and that would cost him severely.

Red swayed to the left, rolling with the punch, then bounced back to the right side and delivered a crushing right hook that landed in Grande's ribs like a sack of bricks. Grande felt and heard the cracking of three of his ribs from the punch, but Red's fury of punches had just begun. The first punch leaned Grande to the left from the pain, and Red wasted no time in bouncing back to the other side to deliver another rib-splitting blow to Grande's body, almost bringing the giant down to size. Grande had never felt pain like that before, and from the look on El Capitan's face, he knew it was over, especially when he saw Red cock his right arm back and deliver an overhand right to the chin of Grande, almost breaking his jaw. The giant fell forward like a tree in the woods and landed face first on the ground at Red's feet, unconscious. Red bounced around like a boxer in the ring, smiling.

No'fere and Sam just laughed; they'd known all along that Grande was no match for Red.

"Nice doing business with you!" Red said, picking his coat up off the ground and heading toward the van he had driven in. Sam closed the back of the armored truck and jumped in, ready to lead the way. Within seconds, the vehicles were on their way out of the garage. The back doors of the white van were still open, and No'fere held the AK with one hand and chucked the bosses and their sons the deuces with the other.

As soon as the truck and the van were out of sight, the two bosses quickly moved toward their sons, who were on their knees like they were hurting, clutching their stomachs. They helped the boys to their feet and embraced them, not caring about the money any longer.

"Are you okay?" El Capitan demanded of his son, who was in agony from his embrace.

"I-I don't know. I woke up this morning with my stomach hurting like this," Junior replied, lifting up his shirt with the one hand he had left.

"Mine two!" Little Carmine added, lifting his shirt as well.

The bosses didn't understand what they were seeing. Surgical staples ran up their boys' stomachs, from their waists to their lower chests, as if they'd been cut open.

"What the fuck?" Carmine said, disgusted.

The bosses' minds quickly turned back toward revenge, but a ringing noise instantly caught there attention, coming from their sons' midsections. The boys' eyes grew big because they were confused at that ringing coming from inside their wounds. The fathers knew at that point that they'd been had—and in the worst way.

"Booooomb!" Carmine yelled, but it was the last word he would utter before the explosives that had been surgically placed inside their sons' stomachs went off, turning the warehouse and everybody inside it into permanent parking lot.

* * *

It was Christmas Eve, and they were $40 million richer, but instead of being out blowing money, Red, No'fere, Sam, and even the Professor were in their shooting range at the warehouse, doing what they did best: smoking weed, shooting guns, and talking shit.

"Professor, you ain't gon' hit shit," No'fere teased as the Professor looked down the lane at his target.

The Professor was dressed in a white smock, and he had a MAC-10 machinegun in his hands. He pulled the trigger, and the rapid fire and power of the gun made him spray everything but the target.

"Just let go of the trigger!" Red yelled over the gunfire, trying not to laugh at the Professor, who was now shooting the ceiling while still trying to control the gun.

The Professor finally ran out of ammo and stood there with his glasses crooked on his face, holding the smoking gun. "What?" he said when he noticed everyone laughing at him.

"Man, brother, I'm gon' see you on the other side, ya dig?" Sam said, still trying to stop from laughing as he gave Red a powerful handshake, like they were arm wrestling in the air.

"You know it," Red replied.

When they released their grip, Sam turned around and grabbed two black bags, each containing a million dollars. "See you later, sucka," Sam said, and everybody in the room knew who he was talking to.

"I got yo' sucka," No'fere replied, laughing as Sam

walked out of the room. No'fere was ready to shoot his M-16, still laughing at the Professor and Sam, with a big blunt hanging out his lips. "Let me show y'all how to do this shit," he said, but his phone ringing in his pocket stopped him.

"Hurry the fuck up, nigga," Red said, messing with his son, who had answered his phone.

"I need to see you now!" Michelle Ramos said through the other end of the phone.

No'fere didn't even get the chance to respond before she hung up. He put his phone in his pocket and continued to shoot the M-16, as if the call wasn't as serious as she made it sound. He knew in his mind, though, that it had to be urgent, because she never called him. After shooting a couple more guns with his father, knowing their time together was limited, No'fere knew it was time to go. 'Pops, I'm out of here. I got some hoes waiting on me!"

"Whatever, nigga. You ain't got no hoes," Red replied. He knew his son was a force to be reckoned with when it came to the ladies, but it wouldn't be right if he didn't mess with his boy. "Make sure you put your cousin money up, boy!" Red reminded him, talking about the $4 million he had gave them to split; it was the perfect Christmas gift.

"A'ight, Pops!" No'fere said, giving his dad that million-dollar smile. "Professor, take your old ass to sleep," No'fere said, making them laugh on his way out the door, especially since the Professor was drunk and digging through a case of rifles.

"Professor, you got that for me?" Red asked, taking the old man's attention away from the guns, before he killed them both.

"Oh, yes, yes, I got it right here," the Professor said, putting down a rifle he was looking at so he could reach in his pocket and pull out a vile of ketamine, along with a brand new syringe.

"Cool," Red said, pausing to put the little jar and the syringe in his pocket. Red was getting ready to walk away, but he stopped, worried the Professor might shoot his drunk self if he was left in there alone. "You got some new weed in the garden?" Red asked, knowing how much the Professor loved to show off his harvest.

"Yep! Sure do! I call it AK-47," the Professor replied proudly and quickly, forgetting about the guns. He led Red to his workshop.

Red took a sigh of relief. He needed some strong reefah anyway, especially considering where he was headed that night. It had been years, but finally, he was going back home. The master plan was in full swing, and there was no turning back for him or anyone who was involved. *Blood in, blood out,* he thought as he continued to follow the Professor, with his devilish gold grin on his face.

* * *

It had been an hour and a half since No'fere had received the phone call from his girl. When he finally walked in the door, he saw her standing there in a pair of black business slacks, a matching jacket, and a white blouse that looked like her breasts were going to bust the buttons any second. "I don't know that girl, mami," No'fere said, pleading his case and thinking it had to be about a female.

"Unfortunately, Fere this not about any of your hoes!" she snapped back. "But I can guarantee you do know this female!" she said, walking closer to him and passing him a manila envelope.

No'fere quickly grabbed it and opened it, only to find some surveillance-type photos, most of them clearly showing Tish in action.

"This Detective Dooly brought this to me and said he can prove the girl in the photos is some kind of serial killer, responsible for the killing of the marshals back at the Waltz Hotel. When I asked him what proof he has, he told me he has a witness but is keeping them on ice till after the holidays. Says he's going to the federal courthouse to try and get a federal warrant for her arrest," Ms. Ramos said, looking at No'fere like she was nervous.

"Calm down, baby. I got everything under control," No'fere said, maintaining his cool composure. He knew it could be a problem and a blessing at the same time.

Michelle just smiled, loving her man's calmness under pressure. It made her pussy wet instantly, but she kept herself under control, knowing this was not the time. *"This pussy will definitely be waiting on you,"* she said with her eyes.

No'fere received the message loud and clear as he blew

her a kiss before he turned around on his way out the door, going to find Tish.

* * *

Tish normally would've been with her family on Christmas Eve, but ever since she'd infiltrated the Reaper's death squad months earlier, she'd had no choice but to keep distance from her family and stay at her secret house on the lake, as she didn't want the Reaper to get suspicious about who she really was. Unfortunately, spending all that time alone had taken a toll on her, especially with her personality disorder, and the medication she had been taking wasn't even working.

Her thirst to kill rapists and pedophiles was far greater than she could have ever imagined, and she now knew that for all of those years, her split personality known as Aisha was nothing more than a means to hide her own pain and deliver vengeance upon those most deserving. Only a couple weeks ago, she'd started having nightmares, but in those horrible dreams, she began to unravel the answers. Night after night, visions of her victims started crowding her dreams. Their bloody, tortured bodies played through her mind like a movie, but the one thing noticed most of all was the branding on her victims. In each one of them, she carved hash marks, keeping tally until she got to five, then starting over again. She still couldn't believe she'd seen at least six or seven number fives; that meant she'd killed nearly forty people.

She held her head down in front of the bathroom mirror, and tears rolled through her mascara and down her face, leaving what looked like black teardrops dripping in the sink. Tish was afraid to look in the mirror, for she thought she might see a monster. As she slowly lifted her head, she kept her eyes closed, but when she finally found the courage to open them, she couldn't believe what she saw. "Fere!" she said, looking at No'fere's reflection in the mirror.

He was standing in the bathroom doorway behind her, but he could see the tears running down her face.

Tish didn't even worry about how No'fere had found her or how he had gotten into the house. She immediately turned around and ran toward him.

No'fere accepted her embrace in his arms, as she laid her head on his chest. He had to fight back his own tears, because he couldn't stand to see her cry, and he felt like he'd broken a promise to her—a promise he'd made the last time he'd seen her shed a tear.

* * *

No'fere was sixteen when Red brought his cousin home for the first time. No'fere and Tish instantly bonded, considering they had no choice but to spend a lot of time together since Red was always doing something.

A month after they'd met for the first time, No'fere had gone to sleep early. When he got up in the middle of the night to go to the bathroom, he heard whimpers coming from Tish's room. "Tish, you okay?" No'fere asked through the door, but he got no response. No'fere just turned the doorknob and went in the room.

Tish was standing there, crying and chanting something under her breath—something that sounded like, "I killed him...I killed him...I killed him."

When No'fere approached her, Tish looked at him like she was in a trance, tears pouring out of her brown eyes. He didn't know what to do, so he stood quietly while she quickly hugged him. Red had told No'fere that Tish had been raped and had killed her molester, so No'fere could only assume that was who she was talking about. "It's okay. I promise nobody else will ever make you cry," No'fere said, holding his cousin in his arms.

She seemed to squeeze him tighter when he said that.

No'fere turned his head toward her bed and saw that her white sheets were soaked in blood. He wanted to ask her if she was okay, but her grip became weak, and she passed out on the floor. No'fere picked her up like a man carrying his wife across the threshold. "Professor! Professor!" he screamed down the hall to the Professor's door, which immediately flew open.

The Professor could see something was wrong. "Hurry! Bring her in here," the Professor said.

No'fere took her in the Professor's room and left her there in his care, not knowing what to expect.

About ten minutes later, the Professor came back out. "She okay," he said, looking at the nervous look on No'fere's face.

"What's wrong with her?" No'fere asked.

The Professor took a deep breath before speaking. "Your cousin just gave herself an abortion...with a hanger."

"What? An abortion!?" No'fere said, looking even more confused .

"The man who raped her got her pregnant."

* * *

That day, No'fere had vowed he would never let a tear run down Tish's face, no matter what she did, and he'd put an end to anyone who made her cry, and now she was crying again.

"I'm sick!" Tish said, breaking No'fere's train of thought and jolting him back to reality. "I've done some bad thing, Fere."

"It's okay, cuz. I know everything, and I'm going to make everything okay, all right?" No'fere replied. He had known about her dark side all along, considering he'd been following her for years to make sure nothing happened to her. "Come on, Tish. I got something for you," he said, wiping her tears away and going into the living room. He had poured $2 million on her floor, and lying on the couch was a brand new M-16. "Merry Christmas, cuz!" he said, smiling at the fresh smile on her face. He hoped to make her happy for a moment, before he had to break the news to her that one of her victims had survived to tell the tale. "Only...can I borrow 100 racksright fast?" No'fere asked his cousin.

"Hell naw, nigga! You still owe me fifty!" Tish said, grabbing her new toy off the couch, cocking it, and aiming it playfully at No'fere. "Speaking of that, don't you think its 'bout time you paid me my money?" she asked, smiling at her cousin.

"Quit playing. You know I got you. Now come show me this house," No'fere said, kicking a small stack of money across the floor like he was trying to steal it as he walked toward her .

"Stupid-ass boy!" Tish said, making them both laughed. She was always amused by her cousin, even after that awful scene in the bathroom.

* * *

It was 3 a.m. when Red finally approached his destination in the three huge buildings of the Marion Jones projects. *It definitely don't look like Christmas down here in the 'hood, other than the ho-ho-hoes*, Red thought to himself with a sad smirk as he walked across the courtyard. He was dressed, as usual, in black from head to toe, his hood camouflaging his identity. He had a Footlocker bag in one hand as he headed toward the middle building, dodging the dope fiends who walked around without a care in the world but chasing they high. Red couldn't believe he and his brother King had planted that seed for destruction right there years earlier, and it was still growing. When he reached the door, he paused for a moment before opening it. He looked down at the ground and motioned his free hand like a cross, from his forehead to his heart, paying respects to the place where his older brother and his mother had died when he and King were only in their teens.

"Hey, you lost?" asked a skinny, dark-skinned boy, running security for the drug trade that plagued the projects.

"Grrrrr!" Red replied, turning his head around just enough for the boy to see the killer look in his eyes.

"My bad, brotha. It's all good," the boy responded quickly, leaving Red alone to enter the building.

Red took the dark stairway because the elevators had been out of order forever. The stairway was almost pitch black as he made his way to the ninth floor, hoping he wouldn't have to hurt anybody en route. The ninth floor was quiet as he exited into the hall. *They probably all know who stays on this floor and stay the hell out of here,* he thought to himself as he stood in front of Apartment 909 and softly knocked on the door three times.

Within seconds, somebody opened the door as far as the chain lock would go. Red couldn't see who it was, but the door quickly closed back, and he could hear the chain on the door coming off .When the door opened, he saw his sister-in-law standing there, Debra Scott, aka Queen. "Yeah, yeah, nigga. Go ahead and get your laugh out. You and your brother owe me big for this shit," she said to Red.

He had to try hard not to laugh at her. Queen's hair was all over her head, and her clothes looked raggedy as hell, considering her part in her husband's plans included her playing the role of a drug addict. Red laughed, but he hugged his sister-in-law. He was proud of her for making it so long playing the role, like an Oscar-worthy performance.

Queen was happy to see Red, especially since he usually just called on the phone. When he'd told her he was going to stop by, she was instantly excited.

"Here's them shoes you wanted for the twins," Red said, handing her the Footlocker bag with two pairs of Michel Jordans in it.

"Thanks, Red. I was hoping you wouldn't forget," she replied, taking the bag.

"This the stuff I told you about," Red said, reaching in his pocket and pulling out the little jar of ketamine and the syringe.

"You sure this shit work?" she asked, taking the needle and jar.

"Yeah. All you gotta do is inject it, and it's lights out. When you wake up, this nightmare will be over, sis. I promise."

"I hope so, 'cause I'm tired of looking like this!" Queen said, even though she still looked halfway decent as a strung-out addict.

"I'm out of here. I can't take a chance of being seen down here," Red said, giving Queen another hug and a kiss on the cheek.

"Bring my King home, Red!" she pleaded, trying to fight back her emotions.

"I will," Red said as he turned and walked out the door. "You got my word on that."

* * *

It had been a few day since Christmas, but Detective Dooley was sure it was finally time for his Christmas present. He pulled the black Crown Victoria in front of the federal courthouse. He smiled, looking in the rearview mirror at one of his witnesses.

The mismatch killer looked more like one of his victims now, with the long scar on each side of his face and another stretching from ear to ear. The doctors had been forced to sew him back together, like a patchwork quilt. If it hadn't been for his accomplice, a frail white girl with red hair, who looked like she was straight from the trailer park, Mismatch would have been dead the night Tish had carved him up like a holiday turkey.

April had been asleep that night until she heard his screams. Instead of heading out of the bedroom right away, she'd peeked out the window and caught sight of a brown-skinned girl getting into a white Benz with a custom plate that read "Aisha." Even though she knew they were serial killers and would probably get the electric chair, she had no choice but to call for help when she saw how badly Mismatch had been injured.

Dooley was upset when he was first called out to the house to check out an attempted murder, but he never would have guessed it would lead to him closing one of the biggest serial killer cases of his career. When he asked April who had tortured Mismatch the way he had, she offered a near-perfect description of someone Dooley had met before, the manager of Club Redlight. Dooley felt like he had hit a double jackpot in Vegas. Dooley had his suspicions of Tish when he'd first met her, but now he had proof, and he wanted to make sure he had a solid case, so he had waited for Mismatch to heal enough to be brought forward as a witness, along with April.

"Let's get this shit over with!" Detective Hill said, seeing his partner just staring at Mismatch in the rearview mirror. Hill was tired of Dooley's obsession with the case, and he just wanted to be done with it. They had many other cases to deal with, but Dooley insisted on going after that one like his own life depended on it.

"What the fuck you looking at, Scarface!" Dooley said to Mismatch.

"The man in the mirror," the killer replied in a raspy voice.

"Shut the fuck up 'fore I shut you the fuck up," Dooley quickly snapped back. "You got a lot of balls, considering you don't got none," Dooley added, making a joke out of Mismatch's misfortune; his testicles were unsalvageable, so he'd live his life like a castrated animal—either behind bars or waiting for the slaughter.

Hill laughed with his partner as he pulled Mismatch out of the back of the car.

They had arrived early at the courthouse due to Dooley's

eagerness. The lobby only had about ten people in it. Some were chatting, and others were waiting on the elevators, preparing to go to court. Dooley was in the front, with his two handcuffed witnesses between him and Hill.

They approached the security checkpoint, where two security officers in black suits awaited them with metal-detecting wands .

Dooley quickly flashed his badge, and the security let them pass.

BEEP! went the alarm because of the cuffs and the detectives' guns.

"I'm looking for Judge Alberson's courtroom?" Dooley asked the white security officer on the left.

"Take the elevators to the right to the fourth floor, Room 409," the black security man on the right replied before his partner could answer.

Dooley just rudely walked off like the man didn't say anything.

"Thanks!" Hill said for his partner as he passed the security officers, bringing up the rear.

Dooley walked toward the elevators like a man on a mission. He was just getting ready to push the button when some commotion from behind him stopped him dead in his tracks.

The beeping of the walk-through metal detectors made the white security guard come forward with his wand as the light-skinned black man approached. He was wearing all black, from his shirt to his shoes. The man hid his hands inside his black hooded jacket, which was unzipped .

"Take your hands out of your pockets!" the white security guard demanded, reaching his hand out toward the man's chest.

The man just kept coming forward toward him, with his hand in his pocket. Then, he said with a smile, "You want my hands out? No problem!"

The security officer was a cock strong man, but when No'fere quickly pulled his hands out of his pocket and grabbed his extended hand and broke all his fingers back, there was nothing his strength could do for him, and he fell to his knees. The pain of his broken fingers was excruciating, and he was in shock at the sight of his fingertips grazing the back of his wrist. His thought was interrupted by the knee that smashed in his nose and knocked the front of his teeth out, leaving him unconscious, with blood pouring from his face.

The black security officer pulled his Glock .45 out of his holster, but the light-skinned man was fast as lightning. Just as the officer was raising his weapon to fire, No'fere grabbed his hand and flipped his wrist back, almost breaking it and causing the man to shoot himself in the knee as he disarmed him.

No'fere looked across the lobby toward Dooley, Hill, and their witnesses, making eye contact with Dooley and smiling.

Dooley almost froze up at the sight of the man's familiar stare; he remembered in that instant where he knew the man from. "That's the asshole from the club!" Dooley said, thinking out loud.

"Move!" Hill yelled out, breaking Dooley's trance.

No'fere stepped over the man who was screaming with pain from his gunshot wound, aiming the .45 in their direction. The detectives reached for their sidearms, but No'fere shot off five shots before they could reach them. He missed everybody but April, whose brains were now part of the elevator door behind her lifeless body. No'fere laughed at the screams of people fleeing from the lobby and at the rest of his targets, who were desperately trying to get off the floor.

Just as No'fere began to take a step, two more security guards came running out from the left elevators with their guns drawn. "Freeeeeze!" the officers yelled simultaneously.

As soon as the word left their mouths, No'fere turned in their direction and let off four shots.

The two officers seemed to crumble at their knees as the bullets sent them collapsing to the floor.

Dooley looked toward the elevator and remembered he'd forgotten to push the button. He looked behind him, but he didn't know where the hallway led. *I guess I'm gonna find out,* he thought, getting to his feet and jerking the handcuffed Mismatch along with him.

Hill shot in No'fere's direction, but he missed.

"Come on!" Dooley yelled, ordering his partner to hurry up and follow him. They barely made it around the corner as bullets hit the marble wall just inches from Hill's head.

As they made their way around the corner at the end of the hallway, No'fere kept smiling and pursued them at a walking pace. He looked over at April, who was slumped against the elevator door. The elevator opened, and her body fell in at the feet of an old black janitor with gray hair.

The janitor jumped back, looking at the dead girl, but his eyes quickly looked up at No'fere, who was aiming the gun at him. "I ain't seen a muthafucking thing!" the old janitor said, holding his hands up.

"Then get outta here, Pops!" No'fere said, waving the front of his gun to tell the old man to make a quick departure and keep his mouth shut.

Dooley had led them into a dead end, with a bulletproof window at the end of the hallway. Through the window was a view of the building next door, and there were men's and women's restroom on either side. "Hurry up! Get him in the bathroom!" Dooley said, gripping his .38 revolver and aiming in the only direction No'fere could possibly come from.

Detective Hill grabbed the door on the women's bathroom, but it was locked. "Fuck!" he shouted, but he quickly got over it when he realized the men's room opened right up. "Come on!" Hill said, grabbing Mismatch and throwing him into the bathroom.

"Go! I'm going to hold him off. Lock the door until I

tell you it's clear!" Dooley demanded.

Hill closed the door and locked it behind him.

"You fucking cops gonna get me killed!" Mismatch said, standing behind Hill, who was aiming his gun at the door.

"Shut the fuck up 'fore I kill you myself!" Hill replied.

The two men were so focused on the door that they never heard the bathroom stall door creeping open behind them, until it was too late.

Mismatch felt an arm wrap around his throat hard, choking him like a python around his neck.

"I thought I killed you already! This like déjà vu'!" Tish whispered in his ear right before she ran her straight razor across his throat.

Hill turned around as the blood sprayed on him and quickly squeezed his trigger four times. The bullets hit Mismatch in his chest, as Tish used him as a human shield. She pushed his body toward Hill until she knocked Hill's gun to the floor. Hill hurriedly pushed the bloody murderer off of him and tried to wipe the blood out of his face so he could reach for his back-up gun that was hidden by his ankle, but his actions were cut short by the two .40-caliber bullets that hit him high in his chest, leaving him dead on the floor next to Mismatch.

The gunfire from inside the bathroom made Dooley grab the door and try and open it. "Hill?" he yelled, but there was no answer. As he looked down, he could see the blood running from under the door. *I walked right into a trap,*

Dooley thought, right before a bullet took a chunk out of the wall right in front of his face. Dooley returned fire toward No'fere, who had popped out from around the corner and quickly popped back, ducking Dooley's bullets.

"You done?" No'fere asked, communicating with Tish with an earpiece.

"Yeah. Now get rid of this pig outside the door so we can get out of here!" she replied while she dragged her two victim's bodies out of the way so she could let her cousin in.

"Listen to me, Tish. I want you to get out of here. Don't worry about me," No'fere said. "I'll meet you on the other side!"

"What you talking about, nigga? Let's go!" Tish demanded to her cousin.

"Just know your mission ain't my mission. I love you, cuz," No'fere said back.

Tish began to reply back, but she became quiet as she heard a voice in the background.

"Put the gun down!"

No'fere stood there, pausing for a second, as a S.W.A.T. team took formation behind him, aiming their weapons and daring him to make a move.

"Come on! Don't make us shoot!" the S.W.A.T. commander yelled.

Instead, No'fere acted like he didn't hear him and spun around, raising his gun.

S.W.A.T. began firing, and four bullets hit him right in

the center, knocking him back onto the floor behind him, into the hallway where Dooley was waiting.

"Nooooooooooo!" Tish yelled from the bathroom, startling Dooley.

"Help! We've got an officer down!" Dooley yelled around the corner as he approached No'fere, who was lying motionless. Dooley kicked the gun away from his hand, flashing his badge toward the S.W.A.T. team as they approached. "Hurry! I think we've got a second perp in the bathroom, armed," Dooley told the officers, who were ready for some more action. Then, he bent down by No'fere about to check his pulse. "You know I'm going to leave that bitch dead, just like you," Dooley said, looking at No'fere. The detective put his hand on No'fere's chest to check for a pulse, because there wasn't any blood coming from his body—only to realize No'fere was wearing a bulletproof vest! Dooley's eyes grew big, especially when he saw No'fere's pop open.

"Fooled you, didn't I?" No'fere said, startling Dooley and making him fall backward on his ass. "I give up!" No'fere said, surrounded by S.W.A.T., who quickly rolled him over and handcuffed him.

Tears ran down Tish's face when she thought her cousin was dead, but when she heard his voice again, her grief was wiped away. She now understood what No'fere had said about his mission not being hers. *No'fere wants—or needs—to go to jail,* she thought to herself right before his words came through her earpiece.

"Is you going to stay there all day, or is you going to wait till they kick the door in?!" No'fere said right before a *bang* came at the door, making Tish jump into action. "It's all up to you now. I'll be waiting!" No'fere finished before S.W.A.T. removed the earpiece from his ear.

The second *bang* made the door come open, but they were just seconds too late as Tish disappeared back into the ceiling and placed the panel back just in time to hide her escape.

* * *

It had been a couple weeks since the incident at the courthouse, and the last two weeks had been long for Detective Dooley. He had been labeled as a hero for bringing down the person responsible for the mass murder of the U.S. marshals almost a year ago at the Waltz Hotel, since No'fere had given them a full confession. Dooley knew the confession was a bunch of bullshit, but he took it anyway, biding his time till he could find the female and kill her.

The rain poured down as Detective Dooley sped through traffic in his black Crown Victoria like a bat out of hell. It was the first break he'd gotten in weeks, and he wasn't going to waste it. He looked over at the passenger seat that his partner used to sit in and quickly pulled his flask out of his pocket and took a swig of his Jack Daniels. He remembered that it used to burn going down, but now it was like drinking ice-cold water on a summer day. Even though he wasn't good at hiding his little drinking habit, which called him day and night, he was good at hiding the real little vice that had tempted him since his partner, now the mayor of the city, had introduced it to him his rookie year on the force .

* * *

It was the summer of '86. Crack had the streets under siege. Police were stretched to limit, trying to stop the epidemic. Nobody would've ever guessed that the world's biggest kidnapping ring was starting, and its roots were right there in the police station.

Dooley's introduction through his partner, Detective Styles came so abruptly that he almost felt like it was forced on him. It was late, and they'd been patrolling the slums of the city all day. Even though it was way past quitting time, Stiles just cruised block after block, as if he were looking for someone. Dooley never asked a question, especially since he really had nothing else to do, but at times he wished he had, just so he could have an excuse to go home.

Dooley had almost fallen asleep when he suddenly felt the police car take off down the street. He raised up in his seat when the car came to a quick stop, throwing him forward.

Styles turned to him and ordered, "Stay here!"

Dooley didn't even get to respond before his partner jumped out of the car, his blond curls bouncing as he walked down the street. Dooley didn't know what to think as he sat there in that dark, empty street while his partner disappeared around the corner. He'd heard what his partner had told him, but it had been five minutes, and he was getting nervous.

Just as Dooley grabbed the door handle to exit the car, his partner emerged from around the corner, but he wasn't alone; a black girl with long black hair and a red summer dress was next to him, holding his hand. Dooley was sure the girl couldn't be any older than twelve, but that was nothing new, since young girls often strolled the streets late at night while their parents were too busy chasing a high to pay any attention to them.

The couple approached the car, and Styles opened the back door to let the little girl in. He then quickly jumped in the car and pulled off.

"I hate seeing these little kids out walking the streets like this," Dooley said.

"Me too," Styles replied with a smirk on his face. "I gotta make one stop before I take you home, sweetie," he said to the girl in the backseat, looking at her in the mirror.

"Okay," she quickly replied.

Dooley didn't know where they had to stop, but ten minutes later, Styles pulled the police car into an abandoned warehouse at an old scrap yard. Dooley was confused, but before he could say anything or ask any questions, Styles quickly spoke up.

"I gotta meet somebody. Get out and come talk with me," he said. Then he turned to the little girl and said, "We'll be with you in a few minutes, okay, sweetie?"

She only nodded her head and didn't say a word. She wasn't scared because they'd taught her at school that police officers were friendly and could be trusted.

The officers exited the car and met around the back of it.

"What's going on?" Dooley said, questioning his partner.

"Tonight, we pop your cherry," Styles replied, looking his partner in the eyes.

"My cherry?" Dooley responded with a nervousness in his stomach, causing him to look around at the darkness of the warehouse behind him. When he turned back toward his partner, what he saw made his stomach drop. He froze instantly, not knowing what to do.

Styles was now standing there with his gun pointed at his head. "Pass me your firearm, Officer Dooley, and don't try anything, 'cause I will kill you if I have to!" he said, not flinching an inch as he held the firearm tightly, ready to squeeze the trigger if his partner so much as blinked wrong.

Dooley showed no hesitation in pulling out his weapon and passing it to his partner. He didn't know if he was going to live or die through the next few seconds.

"It's going to be okay, partner, so long as you follow my directions carefully. I don't want to kill you, but we're way past the point of turning back now. You understand?"

Dooley just nodded his head in agreement. The one thing he definitely knew for sure was that he didn't want to die that night.

Styles grabbed Dooley by his shirt and dragged him over to the back door of the police car, where the little girl was sitting. "I want you to get in this backseat and fuck her!" Styles demanded, pressing the gun against the back of his head. "Now open the door, Dooley!"

Dooley hesitated for a brief second, but his hand reached out and opened the car door anyway.

The little girl let out a scream like none they'd ever heard before. She jumped to the other side of the backseat, trying to get out the other side of the car, not realizing that it locked from the outside.

"Shut the li'l bitch up, Dooley!" Styles commanded, pushing the reluctant Dooley in the backseat of the car.

Dooley froze as the girl continued to scream with fear, pulling on the door handle and trying her best to escape. Then something in Dooley snapped. He wasn't sure if it was his fear of being killed for not cooperating or the arousal he began feeling inside his pants, but before he knew it, he'd slapped the little girl hard, leaving her lips dripping with blood.

"Hit her again, Dooley!" Styles cheered his partner on.

Dooley wasted no time in doing it again. The next thing he knew, he ripping her panties off and forcing his way inside her as she screamed from the pain of the grown man's penetration of her young, virgin body. Dooley was so caught up in his newfound pleasure that he began choking her, losing complete control as he released his load. It got so bad that Styles had to drag him out of the back of the police car before he killed her. Dooley couldn't believe what he had done, and he quickly pulled his pants up and stood there looking at the little girl in the backseat of the police car; she was all balled up, crying and bleeding. Dooley stood there in a trance, like a wild animal looking at his prey, but his trance was quickly broken by the bright headlights that were turning into the scrap yard.

Styles put his gun back in his holster before speaking to his partner, who was now staring at the approaching head-lights. "Come on, partner. Get in the car. Let me handle this."

Dooley wasted no time going to the passenger side and getting in.

Styles quickly reached in the backseat of the police car and grabbed the little girl by her hair, then dragged her out of the car, kicking and screaming. He continued dragging her toward the headlights of the parked car in front of them.

Dooley could barely see what was going on in the rear-view mirror. All he saw was somebody get out and grab the girl.

Within seconds, the car was gone, and Styles was getting back in the police car with a brown paper bag in his hand. Styles didn't say anything at first. He just reached in the paper bag and pulled out two stacks of money wrapped in $5,000 bank bands. He threw one of them in Dooley's lap.

Dooley had never seen that much money before, and he quickly grabbed it and started thumbing through the stack of hundreds.

"Yeah, it's a lot more where that came from. Welcome, partner," Styles said, holding his hand out and waiting for his partner's grip to find his.

Within seconds, Dooley gripped his partner's hand back, accepting his newfound partnership.

* * *

For years, Dooley and Styles had continued body-snatching for profit, but what started out as a kidnapping ring had now grown into a secret society, simply known as the Service. The Service offered specific individuals a chance to live out their sickest fantasies for a price. They kept it discreet, since most of their clients were rich, prominent figures in the United States. For $10,000, someone could buy a male or female as young or as old as they wanted, to use for whatever sick fetish they wanted to live out, as long as they didn't kill them. For $100,000, all the rules were out the door.

The Service was so secretive that clients only came to them by referral, but once they were accepted, they were given a number to call to place an order. Clients were given PIN numbers to conceal their identity, and once they placed their orders, they'd be contacted a few days later to let them know where to drop off the money. Within twenty-four hours of payment, they were contacted and told where to pick up an envelope. Enclosed in that envelope would be a room key, along with directions to the hotel where there victim would be waiting. The beauty about the process was that nobody ever met anybody, and if a client accidentally killed a victim, the Service would clean up the mess for them.

Dooley hated that things had changed so much, and he had turned from a body-snatcher into a client. It still angered him, but considering he'd spent $100,000 for the night, he was definitely going to make the best of it. As he turned into the hotel parking lot, Dooley couldn't stop grinning. He just hoped they had gotten his order right this time. The last time they had messed his order up, he had shoved a dildo so far down the girl's throat that they had to cut her chest open to get it out.

Dooley quickly jumped out of his Crown Vic, making sure to grab his black bag of toys out of the backseat and hurried to the room door. "Room 304!" he said, reading the number on the key out loud. "Yeah, it's time to play!" he said as he entered the room and closed the door quickly behind him. Dooley's mouth began to water as he heard the whimpers of his victim in the darkness of the room. "Don't worry. It won't hurt…for long!" he said as he reached for the light switch.

"How right you are!" a female voice replied.

Dooley hit the switch immediately, but as soon as the light hit his face, so did the straight razor that Tish happily ran from his forehead to his chin, splitting everything open in its path, including his right eye. He dropped his bag of tricks and grabbed his face with one hand as the blood ran between his fingers and pain shot through his body. Even though the pain was excruciating, he attempted to reach for his .38 revolver, but before he could free it from its holster, her razor slashed across the hand he was reaching with, continuing its punishment.

"I heard you were going to kill me!" Tish said before she ran the straight razor across his stomach, slicing through his white business shirt and making him drop to his knees, clutching his fresh wound. Tish grabbed his shirt and ripped it open, popping his buttons across the floor. She gave Dooley no time to protect his chest as she carved a single stripe down it like a tally mark, making him scream. "You know I'm gonna kill all you sick muthafuckas!" she said right before she cut him ear to ear with the straight razor. *There isn't going to be any second mistake,* Tish thought to herself as she watched Dooley's body flail around on the floor, gushing out blood till he was lifeless.

Tish cleaned herself up and left the room discreetly, pulling her little skirt down. She was dressed like a prostitute, knowing it would help her fit in since there were a lot of those in the area, making it easy to flee the scene of the crime. The only problem was her flashy car, so she had no choice but to park far away.

Five minutes later, she pushed the alarm button as she approached the Mercedes-Benz she had just picked up from the paint shop before she'd come to pay Dooley a little visit. She stopped for a second to glance at her license plate, "Tish," and admired her fresh white paint job with the pink rinse that made it look like the car was changing colors and the twenty-two-inch rims that were a perfect match. Seconds later, Tish jumped in car and pulled away.

This time, she knew exactly what she'd been up to and why. She had just killed a man—the first of her thirty-plus victims that she hadn't bothered to block out of her mind. She turned the radio up and began bobbing her head to "I'm Grinding" by the Clipse.

She was running late as the drizzle came down, so she sped down the highway. "Yeah, I'm going to get all you muthafuckas!" Tish said again, still thinking about Dooley and all his sick buddies that she personally planned to visit one day.

Of course, all that was going to have to wait. In the next few hours, she would have the opportunity to break her father out of prison. After all, the Reaper had been paid to kill him, and he had unknowingly chosen her to with him on the hit.

"I'm not going to kill nobody else after this!" she said to herself, looking in the mirror knowing her passion for killing padafiles would have to wait.\ like she was making an oath with herself.

As soon as the words left her lips, she saw the lights of a police Suburban behind her, trying to pull her over.

"Damn! Here go these muthafuckas!" she said, thinking out loud, knowing she definitely didn't have time for them.

Tish wanted to ignore them, but she decide to pull over and try get the situation over with as soon as possible. She smiled in the mirror as she watched them get out of their car, knowing she was about to break her oath.

* * *

The footsteps of the approaching prison guards echoed across the almost empty wing of the prison, where they housed one inmate.

"Tyler Scott, you ride is here," the white rookie corrections officers said, walking up to the cell, followed by his older white partner. As soon as the ambitious rookie got there, he was startled to see the six-two, 290-pound, light-skinned man smiling at him with a devilish grin trimmed in gold. "I...I mean...uh, King!" the rookie officer said like he had made a mistake in calling King by his government name.

"I tried to tell him, King," the older white corrections officer said, shaking his head at his partner, whose face was red as a fire truck. "Roll it!" the older white man screamed back down the tier.

Instantly, the cell door began opening. It was the rookie's first time to meet King, and when he looked in his cell, he noticed that it looked like a high-class bachelor pad.

King ran his fingers across his cornrows before putting his hands in front of him to be cuffed.

As they walked down the tier on their way to the exit, King couldn't believe the day had finally come. For the last ten years, he had rotted away in that prison, missing his family and wondering if the same plan that had landed him there would be the one that would cost him the rest of his life in prison.

When King's lawyer had visited to tell him his appeal had gone through, he knew inside that it had to be his older brother Red who was pulling the strings from the outside. King immediately put his plan into action, using his lawyer to get messages to Red and tell him what needed to be done in order to execute their master plan.

King paused as they got to the end of the hallway, looking back at his cell and hoping he'd never have to set foot in it again.

* * *

The last ten years of my life has been some kind of roller-coaster ride, Tish thought to herself, reminiscing about her past. She thought back to earlier that day, when she'd been pulled over by the cops in their Suburban, resulting in the deaths of the officers and their dog. "Good ol' Peter, the pervert," she said to herself, laughing. *My past reads like a* New York Times *bestseller,* she thought, but after tonight, *I'm 'bout to write a whole new book.* She was ready, always up to a challenge .

She pulled her old Mercedes-Benz, with the "Aisha" plates, up to one of the Reaper's abandoned warehouses. She could see by the look on his face that he wasn't happy. If it hadn't been for those stupid police officers pulling her over, she'd have had time to change clothes, change cars, and get there on time. She got out of her car and into the black Impala that resembled an unmarked police car.

"You're late, Aisha!" the Reaper immediately said, calling her by the only name he knew.

"I'm sorry. It won't happen again," she quickly replied.

"I know it won't!" the Reaper said as he put the car in drive and skirted off. "You know, in all my years being a hit man, I only let one person ever get away, and that's because I was late," he said, pausing as he lit his cigarette and took a pull. "It was the daughter of the man we're going to assassinate tonight, King! By the time I got to the house where she was supposed to be, all I found was this letter!" the Reaper said, pulling a folded-up letter out of his pocket and handing it to her.

She opened it up and she couldn't believe it! In her hands was the very letter she'd left for her auntie to find after she had run away with her Uncle Red when she was fourteen.

"The only person I killed that day was the lady who came home while I was in the house."

Tish felt the rage coursing through her body. She now knew that the Reaper had killed her Aunt Rose, the woman she'd always thought was her mother. Tish folded the letter up and passed it back to him. "Maybe one day you will find her," Tish said. She was ready to put a bullet in his head right then and there, but she knew the time wasn't right, so she calmed down and changed the subject. "Where did you get the car?" Tish said, realizing that the Impala really was a police car.

"I borrowed it from our friends in the trunk," the Reaper said, laughing as he talked about the two dead U.S. marshals who'd been assigned to escort King to court. "Tonight, it looks like we're Jones and Sullivan!" the Reaper said, handing her a U.S. marshal badge and a wallet with her picture in it, beside the name "Karla Jones."

"Ten-four, Sullivan," Tish said, hiding her anger behind humor.

* * *

King had been shackled in the back of the transport van for what seemed like hours. He wasn't normally nervous, but this was a whole different ballgame, especially since he had no clue what Red had planned for his escape. He did know that there was a hit out on his life; one of the guards had given him a heads up after Agent Fellows had come to visit him about his appeal. *Whatever happens happens,* he thought. *It's ride or die from here on out, and there ain't no turnin' back now,* he decided, *just as the back of the van opened up.*

King turned his head and immediately saw the Reaper, dressed like a U.S. marshal. King's first thought was that the Reaper had beaten Red to the punch. The two men stared at each other with a stone-cold stare, but King's attention was drawn toward the Reaper's partner, who was getting on the van. Even though it had been twenty-four years, he recognized her right away. "Latisha," King whispered under his breath so only he heard, and he almost choked up at the sight of his baby girl, all grown up. Red had kept him informed about Tish over the years, telling him she was in med school and was doing fine. She looked fine, but when he saw her wink at him as she took her seat next to the Reaper, he knew right away that his brother had lied about her being in school to learn how to save lives; if anything, it was quite the opposite.

Tish couldn't believe what was happening. She looked back at her dad, and she had no anger against him for being absent from her life. She simply could not hate the man for doing what he had to do.

The three-vehicle caravan pulled out of the prison garage. For the next hour, King, Tish, and the Reaper sat there silently, until they felt the van come to a stop. After about ten minutes of sitting still, the silence was broken by the sound of gunfire outside the van, as if a war was underway. None of them even looked concerned, though, while the rounds were fired off for at least a couple minutes, followed by a chilling silence.

The Reaper reached in his coat pocket, pulled out a Marlboro, lit it, and took a deep pull, then blew smoke out as he began to speak. "Well, King, long time no see. Too bad it has to be on these terms."

"I agree, Sullivan…or should I call you the Reaper?" King replied, remembering the name he had overheard the Reaper introduce himself as right before he and Tish had gotten into the van. "I see you haven't lost your touch for surprises. I guess this is the part where you'll kill me, huh?" King said with no fear in his eyes.

"Actually, no," replied the Reaper. "Actually, I would actually to introduce you to my promising new protégé, Ms. Aisha. I thought I'd give her the honor of doing this one. King, I can't say it's been nice knowing you, because I've never liked you, and I'm going to enjoy watching you die. Aisha, if you'll do the honors," the Reaper said, looking over at Tish.

She was standing up holding her .45 tight in her right hand, facing King. "For the record, my name is not Aisha," she said, briefly pausing. "It's Latisha...Latisha Scott!"

The name had been burned into the Reaper's mind, and he instantly knew he had been infiltrated by the same girl he'd been sent to kill years earlier—the one who got away. "Damn," was the last word he said.

Tish squeezed the trigger, sending a bullet right through the middle of his forehead, making his brains drip out the back of his head from the exit wound. She grabbed the man to push his dead body out the door to make room to get her dad out, as he could barely move due to his massive size. Just as she got him to the door, it flew open, and the Reaper's corpse fell face first on the ground, still holding the cigarette he'd been smoking. Tish immediately raised her .45. At first she thought she was seeing double as she looked at two twins, dressed like bums, aiming golden Desert Eagles at her. Behind them was her Uncle Red.

"Now y'all kids play nice," King said, standing up

the best he could, trying to squeeze in the line of fire. "Twins, I'd like y'all to meet your sister, Latisha Scott!" he introduced, making his sons lower their guns, leaving them with confused looks on their faces.

Tish followed their lead, knowing in her heart that it was blood in, blood out from then on. As soon as her weapon was lowered, she gave her brothers and her uncle a smile, then turned to hug her father for the first time in her life.

G STREET CHRONICLES
A NEW URBAN DYNASTY

WWW.GSTREETCHRONICLES.COM

EPILOGUE

G STREET CHRONICLES

A NEW URBAN DYNASTY

WWW.GSTREETCHRONICLES.COM

It had been three months since No'fere had been arrested and charged with almost fifty counts of murder, all of which he'd surprisingly confessed to. The only thing he wanted in exchange for his confession was to be sent to a federal prison in the mountains of Colorado that housed some of the most dangerous men in the United States—political prisoners, as they were known in the streets. The deal was quickly made by the prosecutor, and off he went to serve his natural life sentence.

Now he was inmate John Doe, considering he refused to tell the police his name. Since he had no priors, there was nothing they could do about it.

In the maximum security prison, they were only allowed one hour out a day, which they spent walking around a little individual cage that separated each of the inmates, all of whom had a violent nature.

No'fere was doing push-ups in his cage, trying to keep in shape. Just as he bent his elbows, touching his chest to the concrete, a voice got his attention. Immediately he stopped his workout and slowly got up.

"All this time, and you still can't get it right, sucka!" the approaching guard said, stopping outside his cage.

No'fere knew exactly who it was when he heard the voice, as there wasn't but one person in the world who called him by that name. No'fere had to stop from laughing as he looked at Sam, standing in front of him in a prison officer's uniform. His afro had been cut down to a fade, and his pork chop sideburns, which used to make him resemble Shaft, had been removed, along with the rest of his facial hair, all except for his mustache.

"You must want to stay here," Sam said, messing with No'fere.

"Come on! Stop playing!" No'fere replied back .

"They ready?" Sam asked, getting serious.

No'fere looked over to his right. Almost simultaneously, two older black men in the next two cages looked back over at No'fere and Sam, nodding their heads like they knew exactly what Sam had asked. No'fere just looked back at Sam and nodded. All No'fere knew about them was that they were notorious rival gang leaders from Chicago, and they'd started some of the most dangerous street gangs back in the sixties—gangs that continued to multiply in number across the U.S., even while they'd been incarcerated for the last twenty to thirty years of their lives.

We'd like to thank you for supporting G Street Chronicles and invite you to join our social networks. Please be sure to post a review when you're finished reading.

Facebook
G Street Chronicles Fan Page
G Street Chronicles CEO Exclusive Readers Group

Twitter
@GStreetChronicl

My Space
G Street Chronicles

Email us and we'll add you to our mailing list
fans@gstreetchronicles.com

George Sherman Hudson, CEO
Shawna A., COO

39669258R00150

Made in the USA
Lexington, KY
07 March 2015